MW01114730

DISTORTED

Five imaginative tales on the dark side

Roberta L. Smith

www.BertaBooks.com

These tales are works of fiction. Names, characters, incidents and some places are a product of the author's imagination. All elements are used fictitiously.

Distorted
Five imaginative tales on the dark side
Copyright © 2012 by Roberta L. Smith

All rights reserved.

ISBN-13: 9781479239887
ISBN-10: 1479239887

No part of this book may be reproduced or transmitted in any form or by any means, electronic or mechanical without permission of the author.

Other books by Roberta L. Smith

The Secret of Lucianne Dove

Chapel Playhouse

The Accordo

The Dreamer of Downing Street

Simone's Ghosts

Bouquet of Lies

Distorted

Five imaginative tales on the dark side

Contents

Bed of Thorns

"I'm sorry I got you into this." Ted spoke off-handedly. He was concerned with locking the door and closing the curtains. Callie watched him anxiously secure the room and didn't answer because her throat was so dry she couldn't speak.

A missing curtain hook meant a paperclip was needed to prevent gapping. Luckily, Callie had located one on the floor. Fumbling, dropping the clip twice, Ted finally got the two pieces of fabric to stick. He looked at her. "I mean it. I'm sorry."

"It's okay," she managed to whisper, her eyes giving the room a once-over.

It was one of those cut-rate places, not all that clean. A luxury motor inn forty years ago, no one had invested in updates in as many years. Now, at forty-six bucks a pop, any amount of money seemed like too much to pay for the privilege of one-night's stay.

She examined the stained, non-descript, gray-green carpet. Maybe it had been vacuumed, but who knew when it had been shampooed. She wouldn't walk barefoot, that was for sure. Her eyes moved to the bed. It was a queen, the headboard a piece of scratched mahogany screwed to the wall, the spread a shiny material with faded blue and yellow flowers.

Callie wrapped her arms around herself. She might catch some horrible disease just by breathing the air. It would have been nice to leave the door open for a while, but that was out of the question.

"I told them I only needed a single. That saved a couple bucks." He tossed seven ones and some change on a table that had seen better days. "Thanks for ponying up the cash."

She swallowed, one hand at her throat.

"I'll pay you back. You know I will." He hadn't paid her back for anything as long as she'd known him which, she conceded, was only a month. His words were a lie. She knew it and nodded anyway.

He moved to her and hugged her. She allowed it by dropping her arms to her side. It took several seconds before she returned the embrace. But she didn't hold him tight. She leaned her head against his shoulder and remained tense. How could she not?

Her mind berated herself. She'd gone for the cutie-pie—again. This time a young cutie pie. He was only twenty-eight, she forty-one. What was the draw? His youth because she'd passed forty? Did she seriously think it was some kind of validation to have a kid on her arm?

He's not a kid, she countered.

Yeah. But he was thirteen years her junior. Did that prove she was still young and attractive?

She closed her eyes, pressed her hands against his back, and held him to her. She sighed. Okay, maybe she wasn't young, but she was attractive. All her life she'd been told how pretty she was. And she knew how to keep her figure.

From where they stood she could see the clock beside the bed with the numbers glowing red. It was 2:51 on a Thursday afternoon and her life had come down to this: An ugly, cheap motel room. A man who was in trouble. Money in *her* bank account. And *her* new yellow Camaro parked away from the room to fool some guy who wanted to kill Ted.

Wanted to kill Ted. Someone wanted to kill her boyfriend.

The absurdity of it hit her and she felt giddy. Was she actually willing to go on the lam for excitement? With a man she hardly knew? Was she kidding? Oh, jeez. When she got bored she certainly knew how to spice up her life.

A shadow passed before the window and an attack of fright traveled her spine. She jerked her head up and drew a loud breath.

"What is it?" Ted turned toward the window.

"Nothing. Someone passed by. I'm just jumpy."

"We're safe. I really think we are." He hugged her. "I won't let anything happen to you."

He was such a liar. She pulled back and gazed into his eyes—those long-lashed, deep brown eyes that had the ability to turn her brain to mush and her knees to jelly. They were grave, troubled, and lost now. That twinkle was gone. The zest for life—vanished. He looked scared and nervous, afraid of his own shadow.

She'd never seen this side of him. He'd always been glib, playful, and fun to be around. Truthfully, she hadn't dated him for depth of character or vows of "I love you." Not valid vows anyway. He said it, but not in any meaningful way. It was an "I love you" that meant she made him feel good about himself. Maybe that was all "I love you" ever meant.

She stroked his face. The rogue had disappeared and been replaced by a frightened little boy. How did she feel about that? Surprisingly, pangs of an intense protective nature rose. Was this her never-been-used maternal instinct coming to the surface? Seriously?

She didn't know what sort of expression was on her face, but the old Ted reappeared. His eyes once again glinted with impertinence and his lips curled into an impish grin.

She grinned back. All motherly instincts evaporated. Her fingers went to his mouth and she traced a line over his lower lip, down his chin, his neck, his shoulder. She pulled off his shirt and put both hands on his chest. Then she tucked an index finger and drew a knuckle along his left bicep. He was so perfectly muscled.

She cleared her throat, her voice barely audible. "What do we do now?"

His grin broadened. "We hang loose. We get a good night's sleep."

"A good night's sleep. Think we can do that?"

"Taking turns, of course. I'll figure out our next move. We're safe. But we should still take precautions."

If she was into precautions, she would have left him already. The person they were fleeing was after Ted and didn't know her from a stranger on the street. She could be out of this situation in a flash if she wanted. Why didn't she want?

"Are you going to tell me what's going on? And I mean everything." She pulled away, but he grabbed her wrists.

"I told you. I lost my head. Sort of like when I met you." His eyes were earnest now. Or, at least, as earnest as he knew how to make them.

He doesn't want to be in this alone, she thought.

"I knew I shouldn't have gotten involved with anyone, not when my life was in the toilet like this. But when I saw you, oh baby. I knew I had to have you in my life." He kissed her, forcefully and lingering. When he pulled back his eyes searched hers.

She felt weak. There would be no precautions for her. She was pulp. She was putty. She was every malleable thing she could think of when in the sights of his cool, sexy stare.

"I know a way we could pass the time," she said.

He smiled again and let her go. She pulled back the spread and top sheet on the bed. She paused. What was she doing? She should run out the door and never look back.

Oh. The sheets look clean.

He came up behind her, wrapped his arms around her waist, held her to him as he kissed her neck, lightly scraping her skin with his teeth. "Let's make love like it's for the last time," he said.

She stiffened and turned to face him. "Don't say that. Please don't say that. You can't believe you're going to die."

"Of course not. And I would never let anyone hurt you." He kissed her cheek, grabbed her flowing hair with both hands and leaned her head back. First he kissed her neck. Then he put his mouth to hers.

Oh, God. When he did that it drove her crazy. She kissed him hard, emitting a low moan. It was like they were both trying to crawl inside each other's skin. They fell to the bed, him on top of her. They had to hold each other. They had to kiss and claw and cling.

"Well, now," a gravelly voice said from across the room.

Ted jumped to his feet. Callie bolted upright, balled hands to her mouth. She failed to stifle a scream.

"None of that," the man snapped.

Callie pressed her lips tightly together and stared. Her heart was thumping with such volume she thought someone in the next room might hear and come to the rescue.

No one spoke and she calmed down a little. Except for the fact that he held a large gun, the guy didn't look like a mobster. In fact, he reminded her of her Uncle Joe. If she were to guess, she'd say he was sixty. He had a full head of silver hair and a friendly countenance with just enough lines in his face to give him character. Somehow that was comforting. He sat in the chair that was nearest the door and motioned with the gun. "Should have used the chain." He laughed a raspy laugh.

"I did," Ted answered.

"I know." The mobster lifted a small pair of metal cutters with the hand that was free. "They still make chains like they used to." He cackled at his own joke. "I didn't want to call attention to myself by kicking in the door." He put the cutters on the table next to the chair. "And keycards aren't so hard to come by."

"How did you find me? I was careful. No one was following us."

The mobster looked flabbergasted. "Hardly matters now, does it? In a few minutes you'll be dead. Unless you give me what I want. It's up to you."

Still huddled against the headboard, Callie looked at Ted. What did he mean? Ted had an out? Her eyes traveled to his left hand. It was shaking, if ever so slightly.

"Why'd you steal from me?" the mobster asked.

"I . . . I don't know. It was an impulse thing. I just— I saw it— I don't know."

"You don't know. You did it for money! And not because you have to pay for your sick mother's operation. You fed me that line six years ago, remember? And what did I do? I lent you a cool ten thousand."

"And I appreciate that."

"Didn't even charge you much interest."

"I paid it back. Every penny."

"You got lucky in Reno and paid me back. Yeah."

"The point is I paid you back. Look. I'll get the money."

"I don't want the money. I want the statue."

There was silence for a good twenty seconds.

"I don't have it. I fenced it and, well, it's gone."

The mobster's face grew dark. He crossed an ankle over his knee and tapped the gun against his shoe. Callie noticed Ted's hand shake faster.

"I tried to get it back when I realized how much it meant to you." Ted's voice had a begging quality to it that said "please believe me."

"You *tried*."

"I did. I offered the guy a grand more than he paid me. But I couldn't get him to budge. And then he disappeared. I don't know where he is."

"Now see. That's a problem. That statue was priceless."

"There must be some amount of money you'd accept in its place."

"There isn't."

"Why?"

"Because I love art. It was part of my collection."

Ted wiped his mouth with one hand. *He's really scared*, thought Callie. *Negotiate. Promise him anything. That weapon is pretty big.*

The mobster continued. "Now there's this gaping hole where that magnificent bronze stallion used to be. It was a Remington. Did you know that? Not a replica. The real thing."

"But—" Callie immediately shut her mouth. She hadn't meant to speak. She'd gotten wrapped up in the conversation and forgotten herself.

"But what?"

"Nothing."

The man stood and stepped toward her. "I want to hear what you were going to say."

Callie's throat went dry. She swallowed before she spoke. "A Remington that was an original would be worth millions."

"So."

"So, I don't believe any of them are missing. They're in museums."

The man laughed. "You know about art, do you?"

"Don't have to know about art to know that."

The mobster's eyes narrowed. "Let me assure you, my Remington was as real as Fort Knox gold."

She wasn't about to argue with a man who had a gun pointed at her chest. And maybe he wasn't lying. Maybe he'd stolen one and replaced it with a replica. Who knew? There were ways to do such things. And this guy was obviously a crook. "Okay, sure. I believe you," Callie said.

The man turned his gaze on Ted. "What's she doing here anyway?"

"We were together when—"

"When someone tipped you off and you ran?"

"She doesn't know anything about this. She doesn't know who you are. You can let her go."

"How gallant of you, Theodore. But that's a question for later. Right now, I want my Remington and if you can't get it for me, then I want something of equal value."

"What do you mean?"

"You can steal something else."

"Like what?"

"He means art," Callie said. "A trade off."

"From a museum?" Ted sounded confused.

"A museum. A house. I don't care. Ms. Art Connoisseur stays with me while you get me what I want. I'll give you three hours or you're both dead."

"Oh, my God!" Callie's eyes flew wide. In that moment she realized the serious danger *she* was in.

"Three hours," the mobster said.

"Something like that takes planning." Callie was scared, but not too afraid to point out the obvious.

The man's expression twisted into a sneer. "He stole my bronze in less than ten seconds."

Callie saw Ted's chest heave. He turned to her. His eyes had that little-kid quality again. "You're a docent," he said. "You work in an art museum, right? Is there any way you can help?"

"Of course not." Callie's tone was sharp.

"Is there anyone you know who can help?"

It was a ridiculous question. Even if she did know someone, they only had three hours. She gave him an incredulous stare.

"I'm sorry to have asked," Ted said. "I . . . I . . ."

The normally cool and quick-witted Ted sounded desperate. Callie's eyes drifted to the gun in the room. Could she blame him?

The man with Uncle Joe's face smiled. "Then I guess it's up to lover-boy, here."

No one spoke until Callie's shaky voice broke the silence. "Okay, maybe I can do something. But, um. It won't be worth a Remington. Not even close, but—"

"Then it's no go, Callica," the mobster said.

"You're asking the impossible," she replied.

"I think I'm being reasonable. I should have just shot you both the moment I walked in the room."

"And what would that have gotten you?" she asked.

"That's why I'm being reasonable."

"Three hours isn't reasonable."

"It's the best offer I'm gonna make."

It hurt to breathe. Callie held herself at the shoulders, arms protecting her chest. Unbearable tension hung in the room. Then the mobster spoke. "Either Ted goes and you stay; he fails and you die. I'd catch up with him later, of course, and make mincemeat out of his good-for-nothing carcass. Or . . ."

"Or what?" Ted asked.

"She goes and you stay. If she succeeds, you both live. Sounds like she has a fighting chance."

Ted gave her a solemn, pleading look.

Callie scooted off the bed. "And if I run, Ted is a dead man and you come looking for me. This is just a game to you, isn't it?"

"Life's a game. One big happy free-for-all." He grinned, flashing big white teeth.

She moved to Ted, put her hands on his face and kissed his lips softly.

"I'm sorry," Ted said, pressing his forehead against hers. "Is there really something you can do?"

She didn't respond. Her heart was in her throat again.

"Three hours," said the man.

"Three hours," Callie said. Ted looked so frightened. He was just a babe in the woods. She grabbed her pocketbook and walked out the door.

◆◆◆◆

Callie's hand fished for the keys, her mind spinning. She felt dizzy. The situation was surreal. She could run, but if she didn't come back, Ted would be mincemeat. And if she did come back, but without a piece of art worth millions, Ted (and she?) would be . . .

What if she came back with something fake? Would Ted's associate . . . boss . . . whatever he was, know the difference? It might buy time. But he'd said he was an art lover. If he did know his stuff he'd probably shoot them the minute he saw it. And maybe he'd be even more pissed off and shoot them so they died in agony, nice and slow.

She dropped into the driver's seat of her Camaro, put her hands at ten and two on the wheel, and bowed her head. She doubted very much the man with Uncle Joe's face would come after her if she ran. Ted was the one who had stolen his statue. He was the traitor here. But how could she let Ted die like that?

She should talk to the police. Yeah, the police. She lifted her head as she felt buoyed, then immediately deflated like a punctured balloon. That would probably get Ted killed too.

Three hours. She had three hours to do whatever it was she was going to do.

She started the engine and backed out of the space. As she drove around the building toward the street, the afternoon looked like any other. The sky was as clear as blue topaz. Birds chirped and darted through the air. A chipmunk scampered across the parking lot.

She paused at the exit driveway and watched cars whiz past. They had no idea she was in dire straits. They were on their way to the store, or to visit a friend, or to mail a birthday card, or go to the show. Whatever.

Who cares? Hurry. Go!

But she couldn't get herself to step on the gas. She was still wondering how she could have gotten herself into such a mess.

Stupidity. One of those walks on the wild side she occasionally took.

But I didn't know Ted was in the mob. I didn't know he'd get me mixed up in something like this. I had no idea.

A horn behind her honked. She came to and pulled into the street.

Okay, she was moving now. She was on her way. Luckily, she and Ted hadn't run far. He'd reasoned that the person after him would think he'd skip town so he'd made the decision to drive only a few miles. An hour away. She was an hour from home.

That meant she had an hour to drive into town and an hour to get back. That left an hour in between to satisfy the gunman's demand.

She looked at the clock in the dash. No. She had forty-seven minutes to satisfy the gunman's demand. Time hadn't stood still. How long had she been sitting and thinking?

She reached the onramp and zoomed up only to have to stop behind three cars waiting for the meter to change green. Two cars at a time were allowed to go. Of course, none of these drivers could read. One. Wait ten seconds. Two. Wait ten seconds. Three. Callie followed the driver ahead of her onto the freeway.

Drive, just drive. Go. If there was ever a time to speed— No! She didn't want to get stopped for a ticket. Or did she? Then she'd have to explain to the cop what was going on and it would be out of her hands. She wasn't equipped for a situation like this, but the cops were. It was their business to foil bad guys.

Her pounding heart felt like it was going to catapult out of her chest and break the windshield.

Just get home and then decide. Or if an idea hits you while you're driving . . .

She felt cold beads of sweat on her forehead. She wiped them away. It was too quiet. Maybe some music would help. She reached for the radio, keeping her eyes on the road. There was lots of traffic. Lots and lots of traffic. She had to be careful.

Her fingers found the wrong button. She glanced at the radio, found the right button, and her eyes went back to the business of driving. So much traffic. But it was moving. Maybe not as fast as she'd like, but she'd still get home in an hour. An hour and ten minutes tops. And then what?

A song blared. Too loud. Too much about love. Too much about death. Too much about bullets.

She reached to change the station and when her eyes returned to the road all she saw were red lights.

"Oh, God!" She hit the brake as hard as she could. The car screeched. She clutched the wheel as the Camaro took time to come to a halt. She let out the deepest breath she'd ever held. It looked like her car was kissing the one in front, but she'd avoided a collision.

She glanced in the rearview mirror. The car behind her had stopped a yard away. Thank goodness. She looked out the side windows. Motionless vehicles were everywhere. She was pinned. No one was moving.

She tuned to a channel that gave traffic reports and waited.

Blah, blah, blah. Whatever was being said didn't register.

"Come on. Let's move!" she yelled at no driver in particular.

Beeeeep. Beep. Beep. Beeeep. The sound announcing traffic finally reached her ears.

"Sigalert on the five. A fatality near the Los Feliz exit south. Police and an ambulance are already on the scene. All lanes are blocked and traffic is backed up for three miles. Police are working . . ."

Callie's mind blanked out the rest. She was stuck until who-knew-when. What could she do? She grabbed her cell phone and punched in Ted's number. It rang, but no one picked up. Why didn't the man allow Ted to answer his phone? She needed to explain that she had to have more time.

Cars began to crawl. How far was it to the next off ramp? How far! She'd get off. She'd drive back. She'd explain. She'd beg. If the man really wanted her to do as he asked, he'd give her more time. The traffic wasn't her fault. None of this was her fault.

"Move it!" she screamed. "Just go!"

Go where? Yeah. Go where? Tears spilled from her eyes.

Callie sat in her car and stared at the door to the motel room. She looked at her watch. It was twenty after six. She was twenty minutes late and, of course, she didn't have the goods. Was Ted inside? Was he dead behind the door? Was the man with the gun still around? If he was and she went in, would he shoot her?

She tightened her grip on the keycard. She was about to do the bravest thing she'd ever done—or the stupidest. She stepped out of the car.

The curtains were slightly ajar. For all Ted's fiddling, they'd come apart. She moved to the window and tried to peer in. Lights were out and the opening was only an inch wide. Was that Ted's thigh? Was he lying across the bed . . .with a bullet in his brain?

Stop it! You can't see. You're making things up.

She moved to the door, slipped the card into the slot. The light flashed red. She tried it again. Red. The card didn't work. She fisted her hand. She paused a moment then knocked.

"Ted?"

No answer. She could go to the office. Find out what the deal was, but what good would that do? If Ted was already . . .

She rubbed her face. There was nothing she could do. She backed to her car and got in. Her breath was audible and she felt hot tears in her eyes. She sat.

◆◆◆◆

"That sigh. I think it's about the loudest one I've ever heard." The man wore a baby blue, button-down shirt and a silver tie. His shoulders were broad. His hair was thick and orderly. He had dimples and a jaw that was square and strong. His eyes gleamed. They were pale ice blue. His age? Too young.

"I didn't realize. My apologies," Callie said. Her eyes returned to the novel in her lap. It was break time. Other docents were providing tours. She'd been at the museum since noon and it was now three. She went home at six. *Three . . . six.* Two of her least favorite numbers on the dial.

Her eyes drifted to a spot on the otherwise clean and shiny break room floor. It was a splattering of coffee or tea, but her mind turned it red and offered it up as blood. Ted's blood. This time she heard herself sigh.

She had combed the newspapers after the incident. That's what she had started calling the experience with the mobster and Ted—the incident. She'd searched the Internet and listened to news broadcasts for mention of a young man's body being found in a seedy motel room. But there'd been no report. Of course, Ted could have been murdered and fed to the fishes, his body never to be found. A classic mob death-and-disposal. Would they have encased his shoes in concrete? She shivered. She hated the thought.

"That must be some daydream." They guy's voice made it past her thicket of thoughts.

She didn't answer. If he only knew. Aside from the sorrow she felt about Ted, she lived in fear for her own life. When would it happen? As she left the museum? When she sat in some restaurant with a friend? That was how she understood mobsters did their dirty work. Quietly. Without any fuss. Someone would come up behind her and shoot. She wouldn't know what hit her. It would be like lightning struck.

Today was Wednesday. Tonight the dream would come. Or rather early Thursday morning. Thursday because that was the weekly anniversary of the incident, her personal reminder of something she desperately wanted to forget. It was always the same—short and to-the-point. She would be asleep in bed and she would hear Ted say, "Why'd you let him kill me?" His voice would be low and calm. She would open her eyes and, feeling clammy, pull herself up. The room would be bathed in pre-dawn gray. Ted would be more a silhouette than a man in a chair holding a gun pointed at her head.

"What are you reading?"

Baby-blue wasn't going to leave her be.

"A book." She looked at him.

He's too cute. He's too young. You've never seen him before. He's another Ted. And you're not interested.

"Funny," he said.

She watched him take a sip of coffee. He remained turned toward her in the chair.

"Sorry. That was rude. It's called *Deadline at Ten*. Don't ask me if it's any good because I can't seem to keep my mind on it."

"I noticed. Your mind's a million miles away, except when you're giving tours, talking about the paintings and the artists. Then you're all business. I've watched you. You love it, don't you?"

"Art? Of course."

"Been at this job long?"

"Six months."

"Only six months."

"Before that I volunteered at the Braden Museum. But, um. They had a problem and decided to restaff."

"I remember. The alarm system broke down and they let it go for what, two days? Someone stole three paintings."

"A Cezanne, a Rembrandt, and a Goya."

"Biggies." The man in the baby blue shirt whistled.

"Masters. Yeah."

"Think they'll ever turn up?"

"There's always a chance, but it's doubtful."

The man got out of the chair and walked to Callie with an extended hand. "My name is Jack, by the way."

Callie felt her heart skip a beat. She shook the hand but immediately said, "I'd better get back to work."

The dream woke her right on cue. In a cold sweat, she opened her eyes. It was six a.m.—the morning equivalent of the time Ted would have been killed. She curled onto her side.

Breathe. Nice and easy. You're safe and sound at home in bed.

She lived in Benedict Canyon, in a house that was big and beautiful and hers. She was the quintessential poor little rich girl, courtesy of a trust fund and Uncle Joe. She'd never had to work a day in her life and, unfortunately for her, she was the lazy sort who never sought a career. She volunteered at the museum because she loved it. It required her presence twice a week. But since it was volunteer work, she could take leaves of absence any time she wanted to travel or do whatever.

She lived a life of privilege and when it got too dull, when travel became a drag rather than a joy, she did something—like date a Ted— to liven it up. When her bed of roses grew boring, she added the thorns.

How many Thursdays had it been?

Five.

The dream would stop eventually. And in time the apprehension would dissipate as well. But until that happened she lived in fear and placated herself with the question, if the man with the gun was going to kill her, wouldn't he have done it by now?

"Hello, Callie."

She shot up and reached for the lamp beside her bed. Was she still asleep? Was this a new twist on her recurring dream?

She switched on the light. Ted sat in the chair, arms upon his knees, head hung low, eyes on her. He wasn't packing a gun.

"Ted!" A mix of elation and shock caused her to freeze.

"Why didn't you come back?" He sounded hollow, sad.

"I did. I did come back. But I was late. There was an accident on the freeway and the car was socked in. I couldn't go anywhere. I couldn't move. Oh, I'm so sorry. I'm so, so sorry."

"I knew there had to be an explanation."

"What happened?"

He lifted his head. He didn't look mad.

"I wanted you to know I wasn't dead." He stood. He looked changed. He was still virile and well dressed, but his movements were edgy and small. He began to walk back and forth. "My boss. Frank. I don't think you were ever properly introduced. He decided to give me another chance." He stopped walking and looked at her. His expression grew harsh. It said he thought she owed him because she hadn't returned. But he was the one who had created the mess in the first place. The parking lot on the freeway wasn't her fault.

"Another chance?" Callie said.

"Yeah. But this time I really need your help. No fooling around." They stared at each other. His expression didn't waiver.

"How? What?"

"Same as before. Only this time we have more time. Frank knew three hours wasn't long enough. He wanted to see if the one he allowed to leave would come back. He got a big kick out of the fact that you didn't."

It suddenly hit her. Would Ted have come back? Or would he have left her there to die?

"It was a big game to Frank, just like he said. But he does want a replacement for that horse statue. That Remington. And he wants you to get it."

"Me?"

"You said you could do it."

"I said I would try."

"Well. You better succeed."

The girl of privilege could feel her backbone stiffen. Why had this become her problem? "I don't know how I can—"

"You work in a museum. And look at this place." He motioned around the bedroom. He picked up a valuable antique vase as if it were a baseball. Was he going to throw it? "You live in a goddamn mansion." He put the vase down.

How had he found her? She'd never brought him home with her. She never showed guys where she lived in case they decided they would make a play for her because of her money. And it was very strange that he wasn't dead. Not that she wanted him to be dead. But why wasn't he?

Oh, no, she thought. What if this had been some sort of scam by the mob to get her to steal?

But that didn't make sense, did it? That wasn't how they operated.

Still. There was that nagging little remembrance of the guy with Uncle Joe's face—Frank was his name?—of him calling her Callica. She'd never met him before. Ted wouldn't have had any reason to mention her to him. Plus. Ted only knew her as Callie.

The look in Ted's eyes softened. The old flirtatious charmer reappeared. He walked to the bed, leaned down, and gazed into her eyes. He kissed her. This time his kiss left her cold. "You'll help me, won't you?"

"Sure," she answered demurely. "Under the threat of death again?"

Ted sort of smiled. "I'll call you," he said as he walked out the door.

♦♦♦♦

"Are you ready?" Karen Bates asked.

Callie had felt like Mary Astor in *The Maltese Falcon* when she'd walked into Bate's office only a week before to show her the pictures she'd taken with her cell phone of Ted leaving her house. Of course, Karen was no Humphrey Bogart. She was a pretty private eye who looked like a housewife on one of those shows—*Housewives of the O.C.* Or, in this case, Beverly Hills. Her office was regulation: Desk with a computer. One of those popular lamps with a green rectangular shade. A long credenza stacked with orderly paperwork. Comfortable chair for Karen, wooden ones for clients. The window behind the P.I. framed her just so. Everything was as neat as a formal French garden. No secretary though. Guess cell phones picked up the slack.

Callie wanted to know more about Ted—and Frank. How dangerous were they? She had warned Karen to be careful. Now Karen had the answers.

"He's not in the mob."

"He's not."

"He's FBI."

"He's what?"

"FBI. Got these shots of him leaving a building downtown." Karen showed some photos to Callie.

"That's him! And that's Frank." Callie tapped her finger on the man walking with Ted.

"That's John Kenny," the P.I. said.

"And Ted?"

"Dennis Wilcox. He's fairly new. Been out of the academy under a year. Can't tell you what case they're working on. At least not yet, if that's your next step. Of course—"

"No. No, this is enough. You've told me what I needed to know. What's the damage?"

Callie reached for her wallet. She would deal in cash.

Callie sat in a gray Honda in the parking structure, dazed. Ted wasn't Ted. He wasn't mob. He was FBI. She never saw it. Not for an instant. She'd been had.

Slowly the sensation of being hit between the eyes with a two-by-four left her and a thought began to ping pong in her brain.

Knowledge was power. Knowledge was power. Knowledge was power.

Yes, it was. And secret knowledge was even better. Ted didn't know that she knew about him and his cohort. She'd been very selective about the private eye and had borrowed a friend's car both times she visited Karen Bates. Ted didn't know. But even if he did, it didn't matter. A smile came to her lips and she started the car. It didn't matter a bit. She knew exactly what she was going to do now.

She drove back to the museum and retrieved the Camaro. She drove home. It was going to take some planning. Lots and lots of planning. But that didn't matter. She was in command and she could take her sweet time. She would string Ted along and never come up with the goods. And when push finally came to shove, she would flatly refuse to do what he wanted. What was the FBI going to do? Shoot her? Arrest her? If they could have done that, they would have by now. They wouldn't have brought Ted in to seduce her. And she'd thought she'd seduced Ted.

She walked down the steps to her wine cellar and chose a bottle of fine red. It was time for a little celebration. Today was the day she had figured out what was what. Next step? Come up with a plan. Next? Execute. And the icing on the cake? The look on Ted's face when he figured out he'd been had and couldn't do a thing about it.

She walked upstairs with her bottle of Cabernet, went into the kitchen and poured a glass. Then she sat at the island and placed her cell phone before her. She stared at it as she sipped. She had upped the home security since Ted's unexpected appearance in her bedroom. She didn't think he could get in so surreptitiously again. But, he was FBI. How did that work? If she told him he wasn't welcome in her home and he came in anyway, he'd be trespassing. Any evidence—not that he'd ever find any—he discovered while trespassing would have to be thrown out. Right?

Hmmm. She was no lawyer. Maybe she needed one.

The phone rang. It was Ted. She answered right away.

"No. I haven't figured out what I'm going to do yet," she said. "Eat dinner maybe. What do you mean I sound nonchalant? Of course, I don't want either of us to get hurt. But it's like I said. These things take time. No. I don't want to see you. Because I'm scared stiff of course." She smiled.

Ted turned on the charm, but she was now officially immune. She promised to meet him for dinner soon, if he picked up the check. (Hey, why shouldn't the FBI pay? She'd paid enough.) They ended the conversation amicably.

She grabbed her bottle of red and her glass and headed back to the cellar. She placed everything on a counter and moved to the east wall. There she switched three bottles of wine between their three special niches in the floor-to-ceiling rack. Then she opened a drawer in the counter and pressed a strategically-placed button in the top of the opening where no one could see. A panel on the south wall opened. She smiled, took hold of her wine and glass, and went in.

A secret chamber in the wine cellar—the stuff of Hollywood movies. It seemed exotic even though she knew such rooms had been around for centuries. She called the chamber her safe room. It served a very special purpose.

Inside, she turned a handle that caused the door to close. She took a seat in a red leather chair and looked at the wall before her. She placed the wine and glass on the table beside the chair. She kicked off her shoes, slowly rubbed her right foot along her left leg, and seductively pulled her hair off her neck.

"Mmmmm," she moaned. "Life is good."

She picked up the wine glass and chuckled at her stupidity. "A mobster who claimed to own a million dollar Remington. I should have smelled a rat right then."

She looked at the wall and toasted what she saw. The Cezanne, the Rembrandt, and the Goya. Oh, yes. She'd stolen them for her own private pleasure. If that traffic jam hadn't kept her from getting home, she would have grabbed one of these beauties and taken it to the motel room to save Ted. The FBI would have had the evidence they needed. They would have been granted a search warrant and all this would have been taken from her. She'd be in jail.

Guess that wasn't meant to be. Their little sting had been foiled by a higher power. The universe wanted her to own these masterpieces; no one could appreciate them more..

"How would you like to be joined by another work of art? Of course, something of your caliber. Would I defile your presence with anything less? But not a painting this time. Something else. A bronze horse. A statue. A Remington."

She took a sip. Wine never tasted more wonderful. Rich. Full-bodied. She giggled and tapped the glass. She didn't know where yet, and she didn't know how, but she'd manage it. Nabbing the three paintings before her had been a fluke. For a museum to allow the security to lapse like that . . . well, she had been presented with an opportunity she couldn't refuse. And now that she had a taste for it . . .

She would not be bored for a long time to come. She had a project to occupy her mind. And when the deed was done, when she successfully possessed a Remington—a year from now—maybe two—maybe three, if that's what it took—Ted and his "mob" boss would know who had done it and they would know why. But there wouldn't be anything they could do about it. Not one damn thing. Because she was onto them and she would be clever and she would plan it perfectly and since the universe had helped her before, it would probably do it again.

The image of Ted and Frank swearing and scratching their heads sent ripples of excitement throughout her body. Ted might even confront her with the truth of who he was because by then he'd know she had played him. She arched her back and groaned with delight. It was such a delicious thought.

And how would she respond? With a demure smile? A faux look of bewilderment? Or would she boldly smirk and pat his angry, cutie-pie face?

Oh, sweetheart. Me? You're imagining things.

It didn't matter what she did in the end. She would have her bed of roses back, having nipped away the thorns. And she'd still possess the Cezanne, the Rembrandt, and the Goya.

But perhaps most important of all, she would have a Remington in her collection. A magnificent bronze stallion. Such a fitting reminder of Ted. And he would have nothing. Nothing at all! Except for a walk out of her life, into the sunset, without a warrant to destroy her, or—

She smiled and took a drink.

—or the proverbial horse.

In His Shoes

Because I'm a reporter and because I write about crime, I knew about the Lindsay case. It was one of those times where the tables got turned. By that I mean the rich guy couldn't buy the result. With his little daughter still missing, the defendant got away with murder.

I was twenty-eight years younger than I am now and was in the courtroom when the verdict was read. I thought the state had proven its case and so did everyone else. The judge didn't even pound his gavel to quiet the gasps, shouts of outrage, and threats that shook the room.

My heart went out to the broken father. He sat stone-still, shoulders hunched, hands sort of prayerful as he stared at the floor. Several seconds passed before he lifted his eyes to look at the man everyone but the jury knew had kidnapped and killed his daughter. I didn't see hate in his expression. Not even when Dobb—that was the defendant's name—not even when he turned from gleefully pumping his lawyer's hand to grin at the bereaved parent. That grin couldn't have been sicker or more belittling. I'm no mind reader, but I knew what it said. *Yeah, I did it and as a reward for a crime well-done, I'm going free. You, on the other hand, get to spend the rest of your days in agony.*

A scumbag set free. Man, had the jury got it wrong. I scribbled down my opinion of the verdict along with a recap of the crime for my readers: Henry and Marta Lindsay had a beautiful two-year old daughter who disappeared, body never found. Jimmy Dobb had a rap sheet. He'd been seen in the neighborhood the night she disappeared. His fingerprints were in the house. But he worked for the company that had installed the Lindsay's security system, so of course his prints might be there. However, there was no reason for them to be in the daughter's bedroom. And another thing. Jimmy Dobb had sexually assaulted his girlfriend's little girl. He'd been allowed to plead to a lesser charge and served no time. The jury never heard about it. Too prejudicial.

My take on the trial was printed in the newspaper. Then time marched on. New crimes took center stage. People forgot about Dobb and his little victim. And for the most part, so did I.

My interest in Jimmy Dobb's lawyer, Mr. Wayne Yeager, was a different story. I followed his career with great interest. He appeared to be a very high-minded individual. Yes, he took the cases of wealthy men. Wealthy, guilty men because that was his bread and butter and it made him rich. But in between he represented the poor and disadvantaged. And he won acquittals. I can't think of a single case he lost in the six years before Jimmy Dobb's trial or the three years after. It was like he was born with a pocketful of get-away-with-murder passes that he loved to distribute. The crimes of the people he set free ran the gamut: Arson. Bank robbery. Home invasion. Drug running. Kidnapping. Rape. Murder. You name it. If the accused fit some criteria Wayne Yeager had in his head, he defended the guy with every ploy in his bag of magic tricks.

I don't mind telling you, it made me sick. He freed dangerous people to wreak havoc on future unsuspecting souls. I wrote about it. Not because I believed my little stories would do any good, but because it simply made me feel better.

Then one day I noticed a change in Mr. Yeager's modus operandi. He lost the case of a wealthy man accused of murdering his aunt for an inheritance. And then he lost another. And then, another. Finally, after losing case after case, he dropped from sight, surfacing only on occasion to represent a client even I could believe was being railroaded. These innocents, he got off.

After Mr. Yeager changed, I quit following his career. I was glad he'd seen the light and even allowed a smug part of me to think my stories had something to do with it. I put him out of my mind and for years he never entered my head. And then, last week, he contacted me with a request to meet.

I was flabbergasted. Floored. Shocked! Naturally I said yes. I wrote down the address he gave me and when I arrived was surprised to find our rendezvous spot was a mental health facility. I thought he must have a client here and was in need of publicity to help shore up his case. But no. That wasn't it. He was a patient. He'd checked himself in and had been there a week.

We met in the garden. A lovely, beautiful, peaceful area where flowers rioted in every color. We sat at a table under a warm, mellow sun, and the water of a small fountain splashed nearby. We didn't shake hands. When he didn't offer his, something told me not to offer mine.

He wasn't the man I remembered. A man who had been animated, passionate, and forceful. Who'd dominated the courtroom with an imposing stance. This man's eyes were hollow and listless, stuck in a face that was large and solemn. He was missing that spark, that thing that made him tick. He looked like someone filled with dark, harassing thoughts, and I decided that something was eating him alive.

"Do you remember the Lindsay case?" he asked.

I didn't have to think twice. "Yes, of course."

"Do you know what happened to Mr. Lindsay after it was over?"

"No. I never followed up."

"He and his wife divorced not long after the trial. You know, she was so distraught she never even made it to the courtroom."

"I was aware of that."

"He remarried a few years later. A woman with a little girl." He paused.

Replacing the daughter he'd lost, I thought.

He continued. "Unlike the families of other victims, he never threatened to eviscerate me, to harm me in any way. In fact, I never heard from him. He just went on with his life."

"I guess that was all you left for him."

Wayne Yeager sighed and his eyes went to the ground. He reminded me of Mr. Lindsay after the verdict had been read.

"I used to represent people nobody liked. The people likely to get convicted for the wrong reasons. I thought of them as the downtrodden and, guilty or not, I wanted them to get the best defense there was. Usually that meant manipulation and exploiting technicalities. I gave no thought to the cost to future victims. It was the law that counted, not the people the law was meant to protect." He looked at me. "You used to skewer me for that."

"I couldn't help myself."

"I laughed at your simplemindedness."

My ears burned. Yes, my thought was uncomplicated: You hurt someone, you shouldn't be out to do it again. If sophistication meant believing that was wrong, okay, I'd be a simpleton. "You seem to have had a change of heart," I said. "Are you simpleminded now?"

He shook his head. "If anything, my thinking has become more complex. I started to question what was true. What was right and what was wrong. Ultimately I took a different approach to the law. Clients I *knew* were innocent, I got off. Clients I *knew* were guilty, I either lost their case or plead them out. And I always made sure they got their fair share of jail time."

"That sounds unethical."

"It is. But is it wrong?"

I opened my mouth to answer and he cut me off.

"I didn't ask you here to debate the question. Jimmy Dobb. Are you aware of what happened to him?"

"No."

He paused a moment before he spoke. "He became my next-door neighbor."

If he'd meant to shock me, he'd succeeded. How in the world could this be? Yeager was upper crust. He lived, no doubt, in a posh neighborhood. Jimmy Dobb didn't have a dime to his name.

Yeager shrugged. "About three years after his acquittal."

"Did that bother you?"

"Did it bother me? A man with no money is able to buy a million dollar house. A man capable of kidnap and murder. A pedophile. I had a wife and a little girl."

We stared at each other.

"I know what you're thinking. He had to become someone's neighbor. Since I'd set him free, it's ironic and fitting that he moved next door to me." He got a faraway look in his eye. "My baby's name was Amanda. We called her Mandy." He swallowed and I saw his eyes start to glisten.

"What happened?"

"Nothing for a while. He waved when he saw me, always with that annoying smirk of his. That was it. I couldn't understand why he was there. I figured someone had to have bought the place for him. Someone with assets and a grudge against me. It certainly wasn't a coincidence that we became neighbors."

"Henry Lindsay?"

"That was my thought. But if he had, he'd covered his tracks well. I couldn't prove it. And, anyway, even if he had bought that house and installed Dobb inside, he hadn't broken any laws."

"Pretty smooth on his part."

"I thought about moving, but I was too busy. I liked my home. There were high fences and security was top notch."

Silence for a while.

"My wife didn't see things that way. After three months, she moved in with her mother. Took Mandy with her. So I said okay, let's find another place. She could look while I worked. And then the unthinkable happened. Someone kidnapped our child."

I frowned. I'd never heard about this. "Dobb?"

"Probably. No proof though. Claimed he didn't know anything about it. Had an alibi and no trace of Mandy was found at his house. I confronted him. I grabbed him by the throat and came close to killing him. He swore up and down he didn't take her. I didn't believe him. Not for a second, but . . ."

"There was nothing anyone could do."

"No ransom was ever demanded. She simply vanished and was never found."

I thought, *Just like in the Lindsay case.* I asked, "Why didn't this make the news?"

"You tell me. You're the reporter. Guess I was simply a run-of-the-mill lawyer to anyone but you, and there were bigger crimes to fry. Or too many of them. I was just as glad no one picked up on the lawyer-successfully-defends-client-who-then-comes-after-him angle. That would have been too much. Needless to say, my wife and I divorced."

"And you changed."

He nodded. "It gave me something to think about. The old adage about walking in another man's shoes certainly fit. I now knew how Lindsay felt and others, as well. I decided I had to make up for them and for Mandy."

There was a tear at the corner of his eye and he wiped it away.

"What about Dobb?"

"He was killed a year later. His lifestyle caught up with him. Tried to snatch the wrong child."

"I guess that's some kind of justice," I said.

He stared at me harshly and I saw the old spark from long ago. "No! He took the secret of what happened to my Mandy with him. I've had to live with that for twenty-five years."

I studied him. I understood his anger. But why call me here to tell me all this now? Why the need for hospitalization now? Had something happened? I hesitated a moment, then dared to ask, "Have Mandy's remains been found?"

He pulled an envelope from a pocket. It was square-ish and thick. He offered it to me with the words, "In a manner of speaking."

I opened the flap and pulled out an invitation to a wedding. Mr. Henry Lindsay requests the honor of your presence at the wedding of his daughter . . .

I looked up, not quite certain what he was trying to tell me. "Lindsay's second wife died?"

"Four years ago."

"And he's invited you to their daughter's wedding."

"I get to bring a guest. Would you like to come?"

Now I was really confused. He laughed, I think at the puzzlement on my face.

"You can write about it, if you decide that's the right thing to do."

"What are you talking about?"

He pulled a newspaper clipping from the same pocket and handed it to me. It was the wedding announcement. It included a picture of the engaged couple.

"She's pretty," I said.

"Very. And the spitting image of my ex-wife."

I looked at him. Then stared at the photo again. I felt a chill and my nerves began to ripple in all directions.

"He sent that with the invitation. It has a little write-up about the couple. See?"

I read and realized why Yeager had come to this facility. "She's a nurse and she works—"

"We've talked. She doesn't know who I am. I haven't told her. She loves her father. Raves about him." He looked lost again. "Do I throw a wrench in the works and tell her she's my daughter? What would that do to her? Why did Lindsay send me an invitation? Did he decide I'd suffered enough and wanted me to know Mandy was alive and well? Is he gambling I'll keep my mouth shut, or does he want me to tell her for some reason? I don't know what to do. What does that simpleton brain of yours say?"

My brow dipped. Is that why he wanted to talk to me? He thought I'd give him a simple answer.

"It's lunch time," he said. "Sorry, she won't be bringing you something to eat. Today it's chicken and dumplings."

I caught sight of a young woman carrying a tray. She was headed in our direction.

"Did you call Henry Lindsay and ask him?"

"Ten times. All he says is, 'Come to the wedding,' and hangs up."

"Mr. Yeager. Don't you look well today?" Smiling, the pretty nurse placed the tray of food on the table and stayed to chat. "Hello," she added, turning to me. "I'm Jane."

"Hello," I said and gave her my name.

"Jane is engaged," Yeager said. "She's the happiest gal on the planet."

"I am." Her smile grew wider and she sang 'la la la la la' and giggled. I saw the little girl in her. "My life is complete. What can I say?"

Yeager smiled at her with love in his eyes. He reached for her hand and squeezed it. She squeezed back. "I don't know what it is about you," she said, looking at him. Then she looked at me. "Of all my patients, I'm going to miss him the most when he's gone." Her eyes strayed to the table. "What's this?"

She'd glimpsed her own wedding invitation that I'd left lying out. I tried to grab it, but was too late. She picked it up. Her mood changed immediately and her eyes filled with questions.

"I know your father," Yeager explained. "We go way back."

"Why have I never heard of you? Why didn't you tell me?"

"We had a falling out years ago. That invitation came out of the blue."

"I don't know how anyone could have a falling out with Daddy."

Yeager looked at me. "He walks on water."

"I wouldn't go that far," Jane said. "But he is pretty perfect." Her smile returned.

I saw Yeager mellow. Should he tell her or not? In today's world he could prove he was her father beyond a doubt. Would it make her hate him? Would it make her hate the father who'd raised her? It would certainly turn her world upside down. What was best for her?

"Are you going to come?" she asked.

"I'm thinking about it," Yeager answered.

"I think you should," Jane said. "If he invited you he wants to reconnect." She handed the invitation to Yeager. "He's ill you know. Or I guess, you wouldn't know. Cancer. He's fighting it. He's gotten better. Well enough to walk me down the aisle. I think he'll beat it. I have faith. He says he will." She raised her hand in a gesture that said she had to get back to work. "I guess I'll be seeing you then."

Yeager watched her walk away. He sighed. We looked at each other for a long time and neither of us said a word.

R.I.P. Katherine Colton

"**I** know it's a long shot. But Beth swears it might be her."

Jenny wiped the baby oil from her face along with scads of makeup she'd worn for the parade and eyed her handsome husband in the bathroom mirror. Mac leaned against the doorjamb, arms folded across his chest, an affectionate smirk upon his face. He teased, "She died in nineteen-seventy. But being such great fans, all you nutcases already know that."

She returned his smirk with an equally affectionate, but snarky stare. "Allegedly died." She splashed water on her face, towel-dried it, and pulled the headband from her head freeing a cascade of light-brown hair.

He nodded. "Of course. The coroner doesn't know a dead body when he sees one."

She held up a hand as she walked past. "No need for sarcasm. Cover-ups happen all the time. Beth didn't say it *was* her. She said it *might* be her." Jenny climbed into bed. They were staying in Harlesville's best motel, a Best Western. It was only a few minutes after nine, but she was spent after a day in the sun and the march down Main Street.

"Every year we come here and every year someone tells you a cockamamie story that you swallow hook, line, and sinker."

"I know." She yawned and closed her eyes, head upon the pillow. "It's such fun to think she might still be alive, out there somewhere in the big, bad world, maybe waiting for the right moment to reappear and thrill her fans. Maybe she even watches the parade—"

Jenny bolted upright and reached for the remote. "The parade!" She turned on the TV.

Mac chuckled. "I wondered if you were going to forget to watch."

"You might have reminded me."

"Nah. I had faith."

She found a news channel, sat cross-legged on the bed, and gave the broadcast her full attention until she realized her husband continued to stare.

"What?" she asked.

"You're a nutcase, but you're my nutcase."

She mugged a face. "Thanks. But I think you're a closet nutcaser or you wouldn't come with me every year."

"And miss the annual celebration of Katherine Colton's birth? Not a chance." He walked to the bed and sat on the edge, eyes on the TV. He had yet to get in his pajamas.

"I hate lawyers," Jenny said unexpectedly.

Mac put his hands to his heart as if he'd been stabbed.

"Present company excepted, of course."

"Well, that's a relief." He wiped nonexistent sweat from his forehead with the back of his hand.

"But look what you guys do."

"Us guys?"

"Somebody decides to hold a little parade in their own little town and once it gets big enough so that the world pays attention, lawyers try to shut it down."

"That's what happens when there's potential money at stake."

"This was just a bunch of people having fun."

"And that's why her estate lost."

"But they didn't lose. They joined forces with the organizers and commercialized it. Did you see all those posters and dolls and watches and junk?"

"Sounds like you should be mad at the organizers."

"I am. Do you know what I heard?"

"No. What did you hear?"

"That next year it's going to cost fifty bucks to enter and . . . and!"

"Yes?"

"You have to buy your Katherine Colton costume from them."

"No!"

Jenny playfully socked Mac's arm. "Yes! I'm coming and I'm going to wear my own."

"Good for you."

"I'm serious."

The news snatched her attention when the in-studio newscaster said, "And on a lighter note, this year's picnic in the park, Colton parade, and cruise of the Caddie's brought delight to many as it has for the past five years."

A 1963 cheesecake photo of Katherine Colton appeared on screen. She wore a strapless bathing suit and an enticing smile—a raven-haired, buxom beauty with seven years to live. The narrator spoke, "Born in nineteen-thirty-five just outside the farming town of Harlesville, Indiana, Katherine Colton grew up poor and dreamed of becoming a movie star. She ran away from home at the age of fifteen and was one of the lucky few who saw her Hollywood dream come true."

A photo of Katherine in a slinky, emerald green evening gown lit up the screen.

"She skyrocketed to stardom after her first flirt with celluloid. A bit part was all it took. But life in tinsel town is not always what it's cracked up to be. Five husbands, a battle with the bottle, and three hospitalizations for treatment of depression saw Katherine's career dissolve like laundry detergent."

A third photo glowed on screen; this one of Katherine entering a mental facility, her hair a mess, her face distraught.

"By the late nineteen-sixties her style and brand of beauty were out of favor. Her sister, who was closest to her, said Katherine couldn't understand the change in culture, attitude, or taste. She grew reclusive and reportedly told her psychiatrist that the world had gone mad, not her."

A forth photo of a white Cadillac appeared.

"In March of nineteen-seventy Katherine Colton was found slumped behind the wheel of her white Cadillac, the motor running, a hose from the tailpipe pumping exhaust inside the car."

The broadcast switched to a video of that day's parade. One of Katherine's famous love songs blasted from a speaker while dozens of women and a handful of men, dressed as the doomed movie star, lip synched and slunk down the main drag of Harlesville.

"Today Katherine Colton's memory is enjoying a rebirth. Every year fans converge in the small town of Harlesville to pay their respects in their own unique way."

Parading Katherines were followed by a 1969 Cadillac convertible filled with more Katherines. An oversized hose arced from the rear of the car and the fake movie stars took turns placing the hose to their mouths before feigning dramatic death.

Mac shook his head at the television. "I don't know," he told Jenny. "But if I were a famous person, I think I'd want my fans to be more reverent."

Jenny crinkled her nose. "Don't think they did that last year. Did they?"

"Yeah, they did."

"Oh, it's just a blast," a parade onlooker told the on-location reporter. "I remember when she died. I was just eight at the time, but I'd watch her movies when they came on TV."

The parade continued with six fans carrying a coffin. Across it lay a large white ribbon with the sentiment, *RIP Katherine*. The pallbearers stopped, put the coffin on the ground, lifted the lid, and looked inside. All put their hands to their faces and opened their mouths à la classic *Home Alone* shtick. They heaved the coffin into the air and turned it upside down. No corpse fell out. The pallbearers screamed.

Jenny laughed. "See. She's not dead."

Mac arched an eyebrow. "Yep, that's the sort of evidence that always wins my cases."

◆◆◆◆

Jenny's stomach churned with excitement and apprehension as Beth parked the Honda in one of Victory Hospital's visitor lots. They got out of the car and walked toward the entrance of an imposing building designed in the Colonial Revival style. It was one of eighteen structures spread over the mental health facility's sixty-acre campus.

"Are you sure this is legal?" Jenny asked.

"You're married to a lawyer. What does he say?"

"I didn't tell him. He'd think this was sillier than taking part in that parade."

"And yet he goes with you every year."

"He's a good sport."

"Well, don't worry about it. We're just paying a visit to an old friend— relative."

Jenny's brow knit together. "Which is it? Friend or relative? We should have our story straight."

"Grandmother. My grandmother who has Alzheimer's."

"What's her name?"

"Um." Beth stopped walking so Jenny stopped too. Beth reached inside a pocket of her tight-fitting jeans, removed a slip of paper, and read. "Audrey Moore." She pushed the paper back in the pocket. "My cousin says she's kind of a zombie, so we don't even have to try and talk." She checked her watch. "We're right on time. All we have to do is sign in, ask for Audrey, and Greg will bring her out."

"What about . . ." Jenny lowered her voice to a whisper. "You-know-who?"

Beth laughed. "Katherine Colton? You can say the name. The sidewalk isn't bugged."

Jenny laughed at herself and they started walking again. "Yeah. Her. When will she come out?"

"Greg said he can't guarantee she'll show—"

"What? You didn't tell me that."

"Oh, she will. Greg says she likes the visitors' area. Comes every day so strangers can gawk at her. But he'll give us our money back if she stays in her room. So we've got nothing to lose."

Jenny frowned. She suddenly felt guilty. Nothing to lose? How about their self-respect? They'd paid Beth's cousin so they could get inside the visitors' room of the geriatric ward to stare at some poor woman who probably wasn't who they wanted her to be. Beth had done some fast talking to get her to go along with this ill-advised scheme. Maybe it was just as well if it didn't happen.

She looked at her "partner in crime." Beth was twenty-two, Jenny twenty-nine, and the only thing they had in common was affection for an old-time movie star. It seemed to Jenny that Beth was more wrapped up in the ballyhoo of fan events than in the admiration of a gifted star. Jenny considered herself a purist—a fan for Katherine's sake—not because it entertained her.

She stopped staring at Beth. They were only a few feet from the entrance. The name of the building was in large wooden letters above the door. Applegate House. It was a beautiful residence, as were all the buildings she'd seen. Each was different in architecture, although they blended harmoniously. The grounds were beautiful, as well. They'd been expertly landscaped and were nicely maintained. A variety of flowers packed the gardens. Lawns were vividly green. Trees provided ample shade.

"It's so picturesque. I'd be outside all the time if I lived here," Jenny said.

"You have to be crazy to live here. This particular building only has twenty-eight beds. Some of the others have more. Most are out-patient."

"So you're saying this woman who says she's Katherine Colton is seriously insane because she lives on campus?"

Beth shrugged. "All I know is Greg says she really looks like her. And if the only reason she's classified as crazy is because she thinks she's Katherine Colton and she really is Katherine Colton . . ."

"I get your point. But I don't think they lock you up for that anymore. Someone must have had her committed for another reason."

"How about, because she tried to kill herself? Huh? How about that?"

"Forty years ago. And the story is she *faked* her suicide so she could disappear. If that's true, why is she telling everyone who she is now?"

◆◆◆◆

A picture window allowed the sun to infuse the visitors' room with natural light. The view through the glass instilled a sense of peace. Walls were white and pictures on those walls were tranquil abstracts of water lilies and koi ponds. Soothing background music flowed through speakers in the ceiling, the volume set so low it mostly reached the subconscious.

Thus far eight visitors sat with patients they'd come to see—two on the comfortable sofas, the other six at three of the many tables dispersed about the room. Some tables held board games. Two people were playing checkers.

"So far so good," Beth said with a grin. She and Jenny sat near the window. Beth's "grandmother" had yet to arrive.

Jenny hunched her shoulders and whispered as she glanced at the people. "This seems disrespectful. I didn't know I would feel this way."

"What way? Places like this encourage visitors. It's good for the patients."

Jenny crossed her arms. "Maybe. What's taking so long?"

"Relax. Everything is fine."

Jenny observed a man holding an octogenarian's—at least she looked like an octogenarian—hand. It appeared he was trying to be cheerful and reassuring while the woman looked downright sad.

Jenny glanced at her watch. "It's been fifteen minutes. Do you think—"

Beth suddenly stood. "Hi Nana Audrey."

Greg approached with a petite, confused-looking, elderly woman. Beth had spoken the lie loud enough for everyone to hear and Jenny felt mortified. The woman was dressed in lavender— Capri pants and a matching short sleeve top. Her hair was white and neatly framed a deeply wrinkled, angelic face. Once she was close enough, Beth took her small, fragile hands, and tried to kiss her cheek. Audrey jerked away and her eyes grew wary.

This is no zombie, Jenny thought.

Greg helped Audrey sit at the table with her back to the room.

"Who have I come to see?" Audrey's voice was childlike. Her head turned from Beth to Jenny and back again. Jenny's heart went out to her.

"Your granddaughter," Greg said, putting his hands on Beth's shoulders. Audrey stared, her face blank. Greg leaned closer to his cousin. "I don't think her meds have kicked in."

"What about Katherine?" Beth asked Greg.

"She's with her roommate talking to some visitors."

"In her room?" Beth sounded hopeful and exasperated. "Why didn't—"

"The *roommate* has visitors. She's not allowed out here."

"Why?" Beth asked.

Greg shrugged.

"She's my roommate too," Audrey said, staring at the table.

Beth eyed the old woman and leaned very close to her cousin. "Why can't we get some private time with—"

"Not gonna happen," Greg answered.

Audrey looked at Jenny. "You're pretty. I don't have a granddaughter, but if I had one, I'd want her to look like you."

Jenny smiled. "You're sweet."

"I'm nuts."

Jenny emitted a sound of surprise.

"Do you have any chocolate?" Audrey asked.

"Uh, yes. As a matter-of-fact, I think I do." Jenny dug through her bottomless purse.

Greg continued his conversation with Beth, keeping his voice low. "When I went to get Audrey and check on Katherine, I was told to get out in no uncertain terms. So, of course, I listened at the door."

"*We* listened," Audrey piped up.

They glanced at her.

"Anyway, the female visitor told Katherine 'Your name is Janet!' It is, by the way. 'You're making a fool of yourself sashaying around as Katherine Colton. She's dead. Don't be stupid.' She went on and on. What a bitch."

"Why should she care?" Beth said.

"Why, indeed?" Audrey responded, accepting an open, rolled-up bag of M&M's from Jenny. "Thank you, dear."

"Go see if you can get Katherine to come out here," Beth told Greg.

"She's not Katherine," Audrey said, unrolling the candy bag. Jenny, Beth and Greg looked at her.

"She's not?" Jenny gently asked.

"Of course, not. She's nuts too." Audrey took a red-candied circle of chocolate from the bag and examined it before plunking it into her mouth.

Beth frowned and turned to Greg. "Go."

Greg shrugged. He crossed the room to a door that led to the patients' quarters and started to punch in a security code when the door flew open and a woman wearing a cheap brunette wig shimmied past. He turned to Beth and pointed, mouthing, "That's her."

The woman moved more like a stripper than a respectable old-time movie siren. Beth sat down. Audrey showed no interest. She kept her back to the room and slowly slipped candy into her mouth. Jenny absentmindedly picked up a green M&M as she watched the strange newcomer put on a show.

"Hello everybody. I'm Katherine." The woman's voice was breathy. She took hold of a chair, turned sideways, and lifted a shoulder toward her chin. She flashed a wide, open-mouth smile. Heavy makeup caked over saggy skin. Katherine's signature beauty mark was prominently penciled in. The sequined gown she wore was form-fitting with a slit up the side."

"She looks more like a very old Joan Crawford," Jenny whispered to Beth.

"She used to call herself Joan," Audrey said sweetly, her hearing obviously not impaired. "These are good." She slipped another piece of candy into her mouth.

Beth scowled. "Greg is giving back our money."

"I'd love to entertain you, but I'm only allowed to sing in the activity room at certain times of the day. And that's when I tell all about my five ex-husbands." The Janet-turned-Joan-turned-Katherine creature moved to another chair, this one occupied by a man. She stroked his cheek. "Hello darling," she said. The man moved his head to avoid her touch. "Don't be shy. I won't bite."

Jenny shook her head. The woman was the correct height and she moved well for someone in her seventies, but she was way too obvious—too caricature—and the eyes were all wrong. They were small and narrow. The nose was too sharp.

"This is embarrassing," Jenny told Beth. "Why do they let her do this? Why do they let her wear that dress?"

The woman strutted to one of the couches and sat. She reached for a magazine on an end table, crossed one long leg over the other and put the magazine in her lap. She opened it and began to silently read.

"I guess the show is over," Beth said.

"Good," Jenny answered. "We should go."

"Not until I have a little chat with Greg." Beth steamrolled to the sign-in desk and began a chat with the woman who worked it.

"She's mad," Audrey said.

"Yes. But she shouldn't be. We got what we deserve."

"What's that, dear?"

"We tried to deceive people, and, well. I'm sorry we used you, Audrey."

"You are? You're sorry we met?"

"No. No, I didn't mean that." Jenny smiled. "Okay. Maybe what we did isn't so bad."

"I deceive people every day."

"You do?"

Audrey nodded and checked the candy bag. She counted out seven remaining pieces. "Most days." She looked around the room then turned her eyes on Jenny. "I don't always take my medications."

"No?"

Audrey smiled. "I take some of them, but not the ones that turn the world to fog."

"You should take all of them. They wouldn't give them to you if you didn't need them."

"Don't be so sure." Her eyes were all-knowing. "I take them when I feel a spell coming on. But I don't need them every day."

A shout from Beth nabbed Jenny's attention. "You! You are giving back my money."

Greg had entered the room.

"Shhh!" The woman at the desk glared with a finger to her lips.

"I mean it," Beth said.

"Outside!" the woman snapped.

Greg's mouth puckered. His eyes looked fierce. He grabbed Beth's arm and led her outside. "I work here," Jenny heard him say before the door closed. She looked out the window and watched them argue until she felt Audrey place a soft hand upon hers.

"I like you," Audrey said.

Jenny smiled. "And I like you."

"I know things. People don't think I know things. They don't think I see or hear. But I do."

"Oh."

"Especially when I take that medicine that puts me in a fog. That's when people talk the most."

"I bet."

Audrey whispered, "Sometimes I pretend I'm in a fog," She went back to eating candy.

Jenny looked at "Katherine" across the room and sighed. The impersonator was reading her magazine, not bothering anybody. "I'm not telling my husband about this. He would really make fun."

"What's that, dear?"

Jenny watched Audrey eat the last piece of candy and it suddenly occurred to her that she shouldn't have given the woman sweets. What if she was allergic to chocolate? What if she was diabetic and went into a coma?

"You look frightened," Audrey said.

"Was it okay to give you candy? You won't get sick or something, will you?"

"Afraid I'm going to sue?" Audrey chuckled softly. "Everybody sues everybody these days."

"Tell me about it. My husband's a lawyer and I hate it when he takes those types of cases. Well, depending upon what the person or company did, of course."

"You're married to a lawyer? Is he any good?"

"Only the best."

"Then I wouldn't stand a chance."

Jenny couldn't tell if the old woman was serious or not until she saw her lips curl into a smile and her eyes beam with delight.

"You're teasing me," Jenny said. "I don't think you're nuts at all."

"Oh, I'm sick. I'm very, very sick. Just not today. Come back tomorrow and . . ." She looked at Jenny and placed a hand on Jenny's cheek. "No. I think I'll remember a sweet thing like you. I remember people I like and people I hate."

"Which category do I fall in?" Jenny joked.

Loud voices carried across the room. Jenny looked up to see a man and a woman coming into the visitors' room through the door with the security code. The man wore a suit and tie, and appeared to be at least twenty years older than the woman. The woman looked like she was in her mid-fifties and was strikingly attractive—a Leslie Caron type dressed in designer clothes.

"I want to stick with the move," the attractive woman said. "I think it'll be fine."

Jenny noticed Audrey turn her head to glimpse the couple. She saw Katherine rise to her feet.

"Bye-ie!" Katherine shouted as she waved. "Come again soon. I love all my fans. Even the ones who are unkind to me." She blew them a kiss.

The man and woman gave each other an exasperated look. "It doesn't matter," the woman told the man. They stopped at the desk and signed out.

"One-hundred and twenty thousand a year. That's what we'll—" The rest of what the man was saying was eclipsed by the closing of the exit door.

Audrey took Jenny's hand. "Come with me." She stood.

"Where?" Jenny asked.

Audrey didn't answer. She pulled Jenny from the table and scurried toward to the door that led to the patient rooms. Jenny glanced over her shoulder at the woman seated at the sign-in desk.

She was occupied with a computer. Jenny caught a glimpse of Spider Solitaire on the monitor.

Audrey punched in a number on the security keypad.

You're crazy like a fox, thought Jenny.

Audrey pulled the door open and she and Jenny slipped into a hall.

"I'm thinking I'm not supposed to be here," Jenny said.

"No. But if those two are allowed in, then why can't I have you?"

"The man and woman who just left?"

"Yes."

Jenny couldn't argue with Audrey's logic and besides, she was curious. They walked down the hall, past several closed doors, all with windows in them. They zigged at a corner and paused when Audrey noticed a caregiver outside one of the rooms. Once the coast was clear they continued until they came to a room numbered 123. Audrey opened the door and they went inside.

"No locks," Audrey said.

Jenny looked at the knob. The old woman was right.

The room was small and cramped with three beds, each with a nightstand. A woman, willowy in stature, stood at the window, looking out. Her hair was long, dark, and streaked with gray. A silver barrette held it clipped together at the nape of her neck. The lightweight cotton duster she wore was pale pink. White ballet-style slippers protected her feet.

"Watching them go?" Audrey asked.

"They are discussing things. I think their life is one big, long discussion."

Jenny stayed put as Audrey walked to the window and peered out. Her voice dripped with scorn when she spoke, "Oh. A gentleman, helping her into the car. And would you look at that nice, expensive vehicle."

The willowy woman glanced at Audrey and then returned her attention to what was happening outside. "They're off. Hopefully I won't see them for a while."

"Who won?" Audrey asked.

"She always wins."

The woman turned from the window and froze at the sight of Jenny.

"This is my friend," Audrey said, moving to Jenny's side. "Did anyone tell me your name?"

"Jenny."

"This is Jenny."

Jenny stared and felt her heart begin to hammer. Despite the inexpensive duster and the passage of forty years, the woman's resemblance to Katherine Colton was unmistakable. It was all there: the heart-shaped face, the wide-set green eyes, the dainty nose angled ever so slightly to the right, the beauty mark on her upper lip that wasn't penciled in.

"Hi," said Jenny when she could get her vocal chords to work.

"Hello," the woman answered.

Audrey poked Jenny with an elbow. "The staff knows her as Dorothy. Ain't that a kick?"

"What?"

"Dorothy. Like in the *Wizard of Oz*. Dorothy wanted to go home and eventually got to. Her sister wasn't thinking when she gave her that name."

Jenny's brow furrowed. What was Audrey talking about?

Audrey walked back to her roommate. "You didn't let them give you that shot, did you?"

"No. I made a big fuss like you told me. The nurse gave me extra medication which I promised to take later when I felt better. Of course, they told me to be sure to eat my candy."

"They've kept her drugged for years," Audrey told Jenny, pointing out a jar filled with what looked like taffy next to one of the beds.

"Audrey," Dorothy said with a cautionary tone.

"It's okay. She's going to help us."

Help you do what? Jenny wondered, but didn't ask.

Audrey patted her roommate's hand. "And I thought my life had become one big fogbank. My spells are nothing compared to what you've been through." Audrey looked at Jenny. "If she still had that private room nobody would know she was here and they could keep her as doped up as they please. But a month ago, sister-dearest decided to save money. So now Dorothy is in here with me and Janet."

"Oh," Jenny said.

"At first she just slept; they had her so drugged. And it took a few days, but ultimately I recognized her. And Janet must have too because she took on her persona."

Jenny looked at Dorothy. It was no longer a matter of wishful thinking. This had to be Katherine Colton in the flesh. "So, you really are who I think you are?"

There was a pause. Dorothy glanced at Audrey and said, "If you think I'm Katherine Colton, then yes."

Jenny's hand went to her mouth. "Wow," she murmured. And then, "Wow," again. She would have liked to sit down, but the only place to sit was on one of the beds. She felt lightheaded and her eyes stung with emotion. "And to think I came here on a whim." She stared.

Audrey said, "I decided I had to stop them from shoving so much medicine down her throat. Turned out that wasn't hard. I used Janet as a distraction and snuck the meds out of her mouth. Once she was coherent, it took me a week to get her to talk."

Katherine smiled at Audrey. "I think I'd forgotten how."

"She had to learn to trust me."

Jenny wiped tears from her eyes. "I'm so sorry. You were such a big star. I don't mean to sound like an obsessed fool, but I love all your movies. What happened exactly? How could you have gone missing all these years? Did you . . . did you . . .?" How did one politely ask a woman if she tried to commit suicide?

Katherine put fingertips to her throat as her eyes took on a faraway stare. She turned away.

"If we want her help, she needs to know," Audrey told Katherine, touching her arm.

Katherine nodded and didn't speak for at least a minute. Finally she turned back and raised her gaze, eyes glistening. "You have to understand how depressed I was in nineteen-seventy. I thought my career was over. My last two pictures had lost money. I'd experienced a third miscarriage only two months before and husband number five had left me for a starlet whose career was on the rise. Then, as if all that wasn't bad enough, my baby sister who had been living with me for a year tried to cheer me up with the news that I was better off without Paul because he had been having an affair with her since the day she'd arrived. She was mad because she'd thought he was going to leave me for her."

Jenny shook her head. As big a fan as she was, she had no idea about this. All the media ever printed was that Katherine's vanity had taken a hit by the changing times.

"I'm ashamed to say, I did try to kill myself. It was a terrible thing to do. Especially to my sister, but I didn't think she'd be the one to find me. I'd told her to get out and she'd left. But she came back and heard the car in the garage. She turned off the engine and got me some air. She saved my life. But . . ." Katherine sat on the bed and smoothed the spread with one hand. "But I know now, she would have let me die if she'd known at the time."

Katherine paused, staring at the spread.

"I had a will, drawn up between husband number four and husband number five, and hadn't changed it. Eighty percent of everything I owned went to my sister. Twenty percent to my psychiatrist."

"The obnoxious twosome who just left," Audrey said.

"I was in a coma for a while and I don't know how they managed it, but they told the press I was dead. I guess no one fact checked or they paid people off. I don't know. I obviously was too out of it to stop them."

"They held a funeral with an empty coffin," Audrey said. "I watched it on TV. And I remember an interview with her sister. She was crying. Great big crocodile tears. Very convincing. It made me cry at the time."

"I've visited the grave. It's in the Hollywood Forever cemetery," Jenny said.

They were all silent, as if in reverence to someone's passing.

Katherine broke the silence. "I had money saved and investments in real estate. It was a pretty penny. They had a lot to gain with me dead. Guess they thought they could get away with it. Guess they were right."

Jenny felt her blood begin to boil. "They didn't just steal your money, they stole your life. They put an empty coffin in the ground and buried you alive. It's cruel and it's criminal."

Audrey's eyes met Jenny's. "That's right. It's *criminal*. And we need to make things right." She walked to the candy jar and snatched several pieces of taffy. She handed them to Jenny. "Put these in your purse. But don't eat them. We throw four down the toilet everyday because that's how many they want her to take."

Jenny slipped the candy into her purse just as the door opened and a voice bellowed, "What are you doing in here?"

Jenny glanced up. An overweight nurse, maybe thirty years old, had entered the room. She wore sky blue scrubs. Her hair looked professionally cut and colored. Makeup was do-it-yourself with too much shadow and liner about the eyes. Large gold hoops pierced her lobes while diamond studs of varying size climbed her outer ears. She wore a number of rings on her fingers and an expensive watch on her wrist. A badge said her name was Liz.

"Dorothy had visitors, I get a visitor." There was a definitive change in Audrey's tone. Mild and sweet had taken a hike. She sounded commanding and strong.

"No visitors," Nurse Liz responded. "She has to leave."

Jenny didn't move.

"Now!"

"Her husband's a lawyer," Audrey said. "He thinks we should be treated equal."

"That's nice. You." She motioned at Jenny. "Out." She thumbed toward the door.

Jenny spoke. "He's a litigator. Do you know what that means?"

Liz put her hands on her hips. "Not really and I don't care."

"It means he handles criminal cases. Wins all the time."

The nurse didn't say anything, but she no longer looked so sure of herself.

Jenny opened her purse and fished for her cell phone. She found it.

"What are you doing?" Liz asked.

Jenny clicked the button for photo mode and snapped Liz's picture.

"There're no cameras allowed." Liz moved toward Jenny.

Jenny stepped back, keeping the camera out of reach. "Now. Now. Touching is a no, no. Could get you in lots of hot water."

Liz stood stymied as Jenny took pictures of Katherine, Audrey, the candy jar, and the room.

"I'm an invited guest," Jenny said.

Liz backed toward the door. "You won't leave?"

"Of course, I'll leave. But not until after the police arrive."

"The police?' Liz frowned.

"My husband will just love these." Jenny sent a text message and the pictures to Mac's cell phone. "There."

"I'm going to get my boss," Liz said, opening the door.

"You do that. And make certain that person knows I've sent photos." Jenny sat next to Katherine and placed the phone in her lap. "I'll wait right here."

Liz stayed put and allowed the door to close. She stared at Jenny, looking nervous, unsure what to do.

"I'm curious. How long have you been part of this scheme?" Jenny asked.

Liz lifted her chin. "I don't know what you're talking about."

"Now see. That's kind of a weak response. I would have expected an innocent person to say, 'What scheme?' Something along those lines. More ignorance and less denial."

"What scheme?"

"Too late now. Shees!"

Liz was silent.

"Nice diamonds in your ears and those are some fine rings on your fingers. Got bells on your toes?"

"What?"

"Nice watch. What did that cost you? Five thousand?"

Liz folded her arms. "It was a gift."

"I bet. The perfume, too? It's called Joy. Eight hundred dollars an ounce. Someone buy that for you?"

"Maybe."

"Pretty classy, expensive stuff. Hook yourself a rich doctor? But I don't see an engagement ring on your finger."

There was a pause.

"How much do they pay you not tell anyone she's here?"

Liz's eyes drifted to Katherine.

"That's right. Her."

Liz shook her head in a burst of energy, a defiant look in her eyes. "Her name is Dorothy Johnson. What's there to tell?"

"Oh, I don't know. How about her real name?"

"Which is?"

Jenny smiled. "Ignorance instead of denial. You're learning." She gave Liz the harshest glare she knew how to give. "How much to help keep her doped?"

Liz stiffened her back and Jenny issued a nod. "Now see? That's a tell." The cell phone rang and she grabbed it. "Hi, honey. Get my text?"

Pause.

"I'm sitting right next to her." She smiled at Katherine. "Did you look at the picture?"

Pause.

"This is going to be one doozy of a case. A career maker, I'd say."

Pause.

"Yes, she wants you."

Liz interrupted. "You know, I just work here."

"Just a minute," Jenny told Mac. "What's that?" she asked Liz.

"I said I just work here. I just do what I'm told."

"That's good to know. You can tell it to the police." She went back to her husband. "Call your buddy in the D.A.'s office? Well, get on it and get the police on their way too."

Pause.

"Talk to her yourself. She can give you their names. But first I need to eat a little crow."

Pause.

"You heard correctly. I take back what I said."

Pause.

"Stop laughing."

Pause.

"Stop laughing or I won't say it."

Pause.

"Are you listening? Because I'll only say it once. Right now I can honestly say that lawyers are my favorite people. The best. You're laughing."

Pause.

"Do you want to talk to Katherine or not?"

Pause.

"Good. Because I think she's ready to talk to you."

Jenny gave the "dead" movie star the phone. "His name is Mac."

Katherine smiled and said, "Hi, Mac. My name is Katherine Colton. I'd like the world to know I'm very much alive."

The Miracle

I don't know how it happened exactly. I only know that when I woke up in the morning I was different than when I'd gone to bed.

It was a miracle, like in that old movie *Big*. Only this miracle didn't come about because of some spur-of-the-moment wish. I'd been praying for a transformation since the age of twelve-- twenty years of praying to be exact--and that's a long time to wait. But now, at last, my prayers were answered. I was her, Kelly Farencrew, all five feet seven, green-eyed, rail-thin, brunette of her.

Actually, I don't think I fully realized what had happened until I arrived for work. I got there ten minutes early like I always did and headed straight for the ladies room. When I caught a glimpse of myself in the mirror I froze. The change in my appearance was amazing. I was seventy pounds lighter, at least. My waitress uniform had always clung to me as if it were made of Super Glue. You know, showing every ugly globby bulge I had. But now it hung from my bones like a moo-moo. I loved it. I was beautiful--model beautiful. I was a perfect size four.

My complexion was perfect now, too, just like in the commercials you see on TV. I'd bought a lot of those soap and moisturizer products over the years and none of them had ever worked for me. But now, when I put my hand to my cheek and I stroked my face, no more sandpaper. I almost glowed. It made me grin. That's when the dimple on the right side of my mouth appeared and I knew for sure I was Kelly because Kelly had only one dimple, not two. I had always thought that was so cool. From the moment I met her in junior high I wanted to have one dimple just like she had. I didn't have any dimples and that was so ordinary. Two dimples were, I don't know, too cute, too Shirley Temple. One dimple seemed so sophisticated. Less Shirley Temple and more, more Kelly Farencrew.

That's when the toilet flushed. I felt my back stiffen and the smile on my face disappeared. I don't really know why I was suddenly so nervous except here I was, a whole new person, and I hadn't realized that anyone else was in the ladies room and this would be the first time I would come face to face with someone.

Anyway, the door to stall number three opened and that wide-assed, blonde woman waddled out. The one who called you. I still can't think of her name and she's a regular at the cafe. I'd been her server lots of times. I can tell you what she always orders: chicken fried steak, three biscuits not two, extra country gravy and a strawberry waffle for dessert. But don't ask me what her name is because I simply can't think of it.

So you know what she says to me at the sink while she's washing her hands? "Good morning, Christine."

Now how could she know me as Christine? Did I look like Christine anymore? No! So why did she say that? I could feel my heart racing and my throat go dry. And it suddenly occurred to me that I'd worked at the cafe for three years and now I was Kelly and no one would know me or rather no one should know me, but this woman had called me Christine. It was very disconcerting, I can tell you that. But then I noticed I was wearing my name badge and oh! What a relief! Of course she had called me Christine. The nametag said I was Christine.

So I watched her dry her hands and toss the paper towel into the trash when she tells me that I'd better get a move on because she's ready to order. That's when she turned to face me and let me tell you, her voice trailed off. There was a look of pure shock on her face and she rushed out of the room like there was a fire somewhere. Well, I figured she had suddenly realized I was not who she thought I was. But I didn't know why that would cause such a panic.

I turned back to the mirror and wondered if that was how the whole day would go. People thinking they knew me then panicking when they realized they didn't? I decided the name badge just confused things so that's why I threw it into the trash. Since I was now Kelly Farencrew, it was time to start acting like her. And I decided something else then too. Kelly would never be a waitress so I would have to quit my job. I would leave behind all those cranky customers who gave me lousy tips and I would walk out of the cafe and never look back. I nodded my head with the motion of a punctuation mark and that was when my eyes went down and I noticed this large dark red stain splattered across the front of my uniform. I'm telling you again, I don't know where it came from even though you're right. Something that noticeable, that big, I should remember. But I don't. Anyway, I touched it. Mostly it was dry. But in one spot it was gooey enough to come off onto my fingers.

So I leaned into the sink and I tried to gather the stained material under the faucet. But as loose as the uniform now was, it wouldn't stretch far enough to reach the water. I grabbed a load of paper towels and moistened them and rubbed them over the stain. All that did was make things worse. The stain was now bigger, pinker and wetter. I stopped trying to wash it off and decided I would just go home and throw the damned dress away. After all, I wouldn't be coming back to the cafe ever again. I wouldn't be needing it. So that's why you found it in the trash. I wasn't trying to hide anything. The dress was ruined. I threw it away.

Now as for the driver's license you're so curious about, that was just part of the miracle too. I mean I didn't have time to get to the DMV and get a new license with the correct name and face. When I opened my wallet it was there. When I'd transformed, it must have transformed. I'm glad too because going to the DMV is always a pain and it's going to save me a lot of time.

So if you're going to arrest me for anything, really, the only thing I've done wrong is leave my job without giving two weeks notice. I know it wasn't very considerate of me and I feel guilty about walking out, but it isn't illegal, is it? I figured they wouldn't know me anyway. They'd think I was crazy, some stranger trying to wait tables for them. Right? So I left. I came home and pretty soon you guys showed up at my apartment. Then you brought me here. End of story.

Now I have a question for you. Can I go? You can see that Kelly is fine, can't you? I mean, I'm sitting right in front of you. As for Christine, she simple doesn't exist anymore. So your mystery is solved and I have things to do. Honestly, you've taken up enough of my time.

Skyglow Undercover

It didn't surprise me when I was asked to go undercover. Well, maybe a little because of what I like to call "the incident" some ten years before—this case where a real creep slipped through my fingers. But then I realized my superiors knew I was right for the job. That incident was a fluke. A blip on my record. So they must have thought they had no choice but to tap me for this particular task.

Naturally I jumped at it. I was ready for some danger in my life. And maybe I wanted to redeem myself in their eyes, too.

I'll admit I've taken two or three lives in the line of duty. Okay, closer to eleven. And I'm very much aware that most cops go entire careers without ever drawing a weapon. What can I say? I liked the action. I wasn't afraid to, you know, get dirty, work the gang-infested streets, rile up a tough guy here and there. In fact, I not only liked it, I loved it. Most of those gangbanger types were sniveling babies when you got them one on one. And when they saw that I didn't care if I played by the rules, that I wasn't afraid to put a bullet in their head if I thought I needed to, and plant a gun beside their dead, scumbag carcass . . . Well, it makes me smile just to think of them peeing their pants.

Now my undercover assignment was vague to say the least. I was to move into this monstrosity of a hotel called the Skyglow where people rented rooms by the day, the week, or the year. It had been built all the way back in 1899 and was sixteen stories tall. Thus the name—Skyglow. Towers reaching into the sky, glowing with electric lights. You get the picture. It was massive, all angles and towers and curly cue decorations. I have no idea what kind of architectural style you'd call it. It was unique and admittedly spooky. I'd heard stories. Close encounters of the haunted kind. But, of course, I didn't, and still don't, believe in that sort of thing. Well, maybe for a while the place had me going. But I'm getting ahead of myself.

So here was my assignment. Move in and figure out what's going on. It was that simple, and that stupid.

Did I ask questions? You bet I did. There had to be more to it than that pittance of a directive. But my boss said he had to keep the full scope of the mission hush-hush. If anyone asked, I was to say I was an out-of-work actor looking for a job.

I stared at him, dumbfounded. And then get this. It was of paramount importance that I move in right away. I didn't even have to go home and pack; they had packed a bag for me.

I climbed into the backseat of a car, between these two muscle-head cops who looked like muscle-head cops, and was whisked away to the hotel. When we got there, I couldn't believe it. They escorted me inside. With all the windows in the place, anyone could have been watching. It was reckless. But that wasn't the worst of it. They went with me to the front desk where they proceeded to check me in. Let me tell you, I was ready to walk out then and there. But I didn't. I told myself there was the possibility they knew what they were doing and proceeded to ask with a slightly sarcastic tone, "Are you going to tuck me into bed?" I may have rolled my eyes. I don't know.

Now the guy behind the counter didn't say a word to us. He didn't smile either. He was about seven feet tall. A giant, hulking

piece of meat who looked familiar. I thought maybe he was a cop
and we'd crossed paths somewhere in the past. I racked my brain,
but I couldn't put my finger on it. So, I decided, a guy that big, if I
had met him, I would have remembered and let it go. But then I
realized that his hair was all wet and his clothes were wet as well and
that was just too weird to let pass. I opened my big mouth and said,
"What's the matter Big Chum? Someone push you in the hotel pool
with your clothes on?"

His deadpan face took on this half-smile, half-sneer—the kind of
look bullies give when they want to show their disgust at the fact
that you breathe the same air as they do. He said, "This place doesn't
have a pool, wise guy. But I'll let you know all about it when we
have more time."

I thought it was a peculiar thing to say and I stared at him,
thinking so.

He handed one of the cops the keycard to my room, still sneering
at me, and said, "Four twenty-two."

Now I didn't give a hoot about the remark or the sneer, and I
didn't care how big he was—I could have wiped the snotty look off
his face in no time. But the fact that he didn't give me my own
key—that stuck in my craw. Who the hell did he think he was?

We started walking toward the elevator and I looked back
expecting to see him leaning on the counter, eyes on me filled with
scorn, but he was gone. And that was when I noticed that the place
was a morgue; there wasn't a soul in sight. Not one. And for some
reason, that creeped me out.

Now I don't put much stock in feelings like that. I consider them
hazy nothings at best. Skyglow was old and decrepit, not sinister. It
had good bones. Nicely planned and well constructed. But it had
become a shabby pit with all of its artsy-fartsy history laid to rest.
Cracked and dirty marble floors. Frayed carpets thrown around. No
pictures. Yellowy walls, the shade of badly-cared-for teeth. Sofas
and chairs were shoved here and there, most with the stuffing
shooting out. The place was nothing to write home about and

obviously, whatever my assignment, it involved the lowest class of person because only that type of person would reside in a dump like this.

We took the elevator to the fourth floor and as we walked down the hall I heard someone whimpering. It was muffled, but still loud enough to be irritating. It came from behind one of the closed doors, I couldn't tell which one yet, and my first thought was that somebody's dog needed to be let out to do its business. But then I heard crying mixed with the whimper and a man's voice begged, "Pleeeze."

It didn't occur to me that we should check and see if the man needed help. I just hoped I didn't have to hear his insufferable cries every time I left my room. It grew louder and as we passed room 412 there came a shout from behind the door, "Give me the shot! I want it now! I changed my mind!" And then came more pathetic whining.

I looked at the muscle-heads on either side of me who were staring straight ahead, acting as if they didn't hear a thing, and I said, "So is it drugs? Am I looking for a drug related thing?"

At this point I didn't care who heard me ask about my assignment. I was sick of the whole mystery aspect of the thing as well as the attitude of the cops who didn't give a rat's ass if I was seen with them.

"You'll figure it out," the shorter cop said and I think my jaw dropped to my chest because I'd gotten an answer, vague as it was.

We came to room 422 and went in and I found the place a sty like the lobby. It had a twin-sized bed, gray-blue carpet, a window with flimsy cream-colored curtains, a long dresser with a small TV on top, and one of those old fashioned landline phones. There was no computer and I doubted if the TV had a hook up for the universal web. I felt like I'd gone back in time. Everything was archaic.

I plopped my suitcase on a stand in an alcove. The bathroom was beside it and I poked my head in to see what I could see. There was no shower. Just a claw-foot tub and pedestal sink. No vanity. No drawers. I wondered where the hell I was supposed to keep my stuff.

The two cops looked around. One of them checked the window. It didn't open. I don't know what they were looking for, but once they were satisfied, they handed me the keycard and left. They didn't wish me good luck.

The first thing I did was open my suitcase. I figured there had to be instructions of some sort inside. I found trousers, shirts, underwear, toiletries, a carton of smokes, and tucked under everything was a sheet of paper. It said to watch the television. I shook my head. This assignment felt like a game.

I put the clothes in the dresser and then I found the remote and turned on the TV.

The first channel was about the hotel—its history, its amenities—if you could call anything here an amenity. I hit channel up and got news. Another press and I got an old-time movie channel. One of those gangster flicks starring Jimmy Cagney played. I clicked again and was back where I started. Three channels. That was it.

I looked at the note again and turned it over to check the other side. Of course, nothing was there. I balled up the paper and whooshed it across the room. Damn them. I didn't like games. Which channel was I supposed to watch? I picked the one about the hotel.

". . . built in what was then the great city of New York. Among its storied guests: Jimmy Cagney (*Ah, that's why that movie.*), Mae West, Jack Kerouac, W. Somerset Maugham, Andy Warhol, John Lennon, Charma Veigh, Lindsay Muffin, John Acosta, David Rohr. To name a few . . ."

It droned on and I quit listening while I went into the bathroom to take a leak. There were no towel racks. Towels were rolled up in a basket on the floor. I grabbed one. It was cheap and flimsy.

Jesus. If they expected me to live in the Skyglow a year, I at least wanted some decent towels. I opened the little bar of soap that was on the sink and washed then dried my hands. I eyed the tub with no shower.

I went back in the bedroom and lay on the bed.

" . . . haunted."

The word nabbed my attention. I sat up and stared at the TV. It had finished and began to repeat.

I learned where the restaurant was. The gift store. How to ring for room service. Housekeeping. Then it went to things less practical.

The voice on the TV said, "Every hotel in the United Socialist Territories of the Americas claims to be haunted these days. But we have been certified by the President's commission on afterlife affairs to be among those sites proven to have ghosts."

A guest was shown telling some lame story so boring I couldn't pay attention.

"Tune in again. We'll have more for you each month. But for now. If there is a knock at your door and you peep through the hole and see a little girl. Don't answer it."

I shut off the TV, ready to go downstairs and have a look around.

This time my walk down the hall was silent. Whimpering Man must have gotten his shot or given up the quest.

I took the elevator to the lobby and as I headed for the restaurant still saw no one around. Big Chum wasn't manning the front desk. Some regular-looking dude stood there as if at attention. Hands behind his back, and his feet, even though I couldn't see them, undoubtedly planted a foot apart.

"Food any good in this joint?" I asked.

"Fair to midlin'," he answered with a nod.

I found the restaurant and was shocked to see it was a cafeteria with long rows of tables and chairs. I felt like a kid in grammar school. You didn't order your food from a server. You spooned it for yourself buffet style, except you didn't get any choices about what you ate and it wasn't all-you-can-eat. A worker stood watching so you didn't take too much.

I spotted only a few diners seated here and there, and decided it would be weird to sit next to anyone with so many empty, nonintrusive spots available. So when this guy in a white uniform sat next to me, I thought it was strange. He didn't say anything. Just slipped the fork in his mouth and smiled at me occasionally. I ate half my dinner—the food was exactly as the front desk stiff had described—and got up to leave.

"See ya," the guy said.

I stared at him. Something about him bothered me. He looked normal enough. Was even good-looking in a wimpy sort of way. But it was like his energy was trying to invade mine. I decided I didn't like him and went back to my room. I watched an old movie and went to bed. Didn't wake until morning when the sun hit my eyes.

It was three days into my stay when I first heard the knock at the door. I had no idea who it could be and peeped through the hole. Looking straight out I didn't see anybody. I almost turned away when someone knocked again. I angled my view to look down and saw the top of a little girl's head. She had brown wavy hair. I couldn't see her face, but knew her nose had to be practically touching the door. She wore a sun dress.

"What the—" I hesitated. What was some little child doing at my door? She couldn't have been any older than three or four.

"Your mamma isn't here," I called.

She knocked again. I thought about not answering, but after a couple of seconds opened the door. And guess what? She wasn't anywhere to be seen.

I'd like to say I'd been napping and she was part of a dream. I'd like to say there was no evidence of her. But I can't. I hadn't been asleep and there were two pools of water on the floor where her feet had been. I squatted down and put my fingers to the rug. It was sopping. I pictured her and realized that her hair, as much as I had seen of it, had looked wet.

"Hey, kid!" I shouted. "Where'd you go? You want something?"

When she didn't answer, I stood up, and that was when I noticed there wasn't a trail of water leading anywhere. Just those two soggy spots. Maybe she'd been standing there long enough to no longer drip before she walked away. But what about when she'd approached?

I closed the door, pondering the kid and the water for all of a minute. Stuff like that can drive you crazy if you let it and I'm not one to let it. Plus, I really didn't care.

The next day I met the housekeeper. It was the guy in the white uniform who'd sat next to me in the cafeteria. He'd said he'd see me and here he was, energy still seeming to intrude on my space.

He got to cleaning right away. Changed the sheets and towels. Vacuumed. Did a bit of talking, too. Nothing about himself. He asked *me* questions. What was I doing at the Skyglow? How long did I plan on staying? What did I think of the place?

It was a crummy, has-been, piece of real estate. What'd he think I thought? I grunted rather than answered and was glad when he left.

Time marched on. I went to the cafeteria for breakfast, lunch, and dinner. It seemed to get more crowded each time I went. But I didn't make any friends and no one struck me as right for my assignment, such as it was. After a month, I decided to have only two meals a day. I was getting a paunch. And then this one evening I didn't feel like going at all. I ordered room service. It was the first time, and wouldn't you know, I had to take a dump right before the guy tapped on the door.

"Room Service."

"Leave it," I shouted. But he didn't. I heard the door open and I figured he had a key. Well, obviously, he did.

Now the door to the bathroom was open, but from where the toilet was positioned all I saw was a glimpse of movement. When I didn't see him leave, I figured he wanted a tip. I wasn't going to tell him where I kept my money, so I told him to take three cigs from the open pack of smokes on the dresser. I mean, they cost a hundred bucks a pack now so that's five dollars each, and since drug companies came up with a smoke that's actually good for you— repairing cells in your body, prolonging life—the law says everybody has to buy 'em and smoke three a day. They fine you if you don't. The thing that bugs me, cigs are still addictive and it's hard to smoke less than a pack so it's expensive. But all this is off the subject.

I finished my business and even though I never saw the guy leave, my food was there and he wasn't. Nobody'd touched my cigarettes, but there was a trail of water on the rug. This made my skin crawl. I had to talk myself out of feeling creeped out.

My routine stayed pretty much the same. Sleep, eat, smoke, and watch old movies on TV. Ignore the housekeeper as best I could when he came once a week. Sometimes I'd leave and wander the hotel.

I started trying to convince my sorry excuse for a girlfriend to come visit me. I know the rules say there's no contact with family or friends while undercover, but hey! I still didn't know what my assignment was and I was lonely and bored.

She only picked up once—after I'd left a zillion messages—and reminded me that we'd broken up ten years ago. She didn't want to have anything to do with me.

"Stop calling!" I'd forgotten how shrill her voice could be.

She was right. We had broken up, although I couldn't remember why. I sat there by the phone, shaking my head, and right then the housekeeper comes in. Didn't even knock.

"You blew it with her, huh?" He moved to the bed and tore off the sheets.

What? How'd he know who I'd been talking to?

"The way you've blown the rest of your life." He whipped a fresh sheet in the air and started making the bed.

"None of your business!" It may have been the first real sentence I said to him.

"That's all right." He finished making the bed and looked at me. "You're the master of your own destiny." He moved into the bathroom.

What the hell was he talking about? I went to the door to challenge him. "What did you say?"

"You want to talk about it?"

I could feel that energy of his reaching out to me. I took a step back. "No. I don't want to talk about it!"

He got down on his knees and started wiping out the tub. "When you're ready, I'm here."

I decided to forget it. That energy of his was making me nervous. It seemed like it wanted to take me over.

It was about this time I finally made some friends, or pseudo friends to be more accurate. All of them lived on the fourth floor.

What got us talking was Whimpering Man. All of us found him annoying. "Pipsqueak"—I gave each friend a gamer name which I never used to their face—claimed he was ready to break the door down and put the dumbass out of his misery. "Preacher" said there were two more just like the guy at his end of the hall. One cried so loud he sometimes heard him through the wall in his room. But, he claimed, he never got mad. He prayed for the poor man's soul. "Motor-mouth" casually said he'd like to punch anyone who made that much noise in the face.

"Pipsqueak" was short and slight and I think he had the proverbial "little man's complex." He spouted the tallest tales anybody could and proudly told us that he used to rob banks. Said he'd killed a guard during one heist.

"Preacher" called himself an inspirational parson. He was craggy-looking, had this long white beard, and his blue eyes were clear as crystal. He told "Pipsqueak" in no uncertain terms it was time to repent. If he didn't, he'd be going to hell.

Pipsqueak's face said he'd prefer Preacher shut up. But Preacher went on and on. Said forgiveness was the answer and he'd help Pipsqueak make peace with God—for a price.

That was Preacher's game. He was like one of those TV evangelists who pressured you to send money or be damned. That's when Preacher said he was on TV.

"Not my TV. I've got three channels," I said.

"I'm on the news channel. You have to watch at midnight. It's called The Midnight Hour." He gave a little speech about how it would save my soul. Preacher said all men were sinners and needed saving.

I caught the program later that week and discovered that "The Midnight Hour" was only twenty-five minutes long. If that didn't say it all.

The third pal I made I called "Motor-mouth" because he didn't talk much. He nodded and gave one-word answers most of the time. He liked to play poker, and we all thought that was a great idea. He had the cards so that's what the four of us did.

We fell into a routine. Cards every night, always in my room. Bets were friendly, penny-ante stuff. Preacher was for upping the stakes, but I wouldn't do it. And when he tried to put the pressure on, I asked him if gambling wasn't a sin.

Playing poker passed the time. And for a few months that little girl quit coming around. Up until then, she'd been knocking on my door regularly which not only did I not like, I found it downright frightening.

Then one night around eleven-thirty she came back. Her knock was quiet-like, gentle because, you know, little four-year-old girls don't have a lot of strength in their wrist or arm or body. I knew it was her.

"Who's that?" Pipsqueak asked.

"Nobody," I said.

She knocked again.

"Answer it," Preacher said.

I stared at my cards and didn't make a move.

Preacher got up and opened the door. No one was there.

"Must have moved on," I said.

Preacher stared at me like he was trying to see past my skin and said, "You've done something that needs fixing."

I lifted my gaze. "No, I haven't. And don't give me any guff about it."

Pipsqueak's complexion went ashen. "Weird stuff happens here," he said. "You know that guard I killed? I've seen him in the lobby."

"Guilt," Preacher said. "Visions. God's punishment."

Pipsqueak gave Preacher a worried glance. "I see him every time I walk through the lobby. So now I don't go there."

"There's no avoiding God's wrath," Preacher said. "You must be forgiven."

We were all quiet. You could feel this tension and then the little girl knocked again. That was when I went ahead and told them who was there.

Motor-mouth went back to his cards. "Little girlie, huh? That's what has your panties in a bunch? Why not invite her in? Quit scaring her away." It was the most words I ever heard him string into a paragraph. Then he cackled this sick-sounding laugh, and I got this inkling that he liked to molest little children.

Preacher did too because he started shouting, "Confess your sins. Confess!"

Motor-mouth answered, "Let's play cards."

Preacher kept at him. Worked himself into a high-energy sermon which at first Motor-mouth took. But then he turned red and he talked back. They almost came to blows. Finally Preacher shut up.

"I am who I am. I ain't gonna change." Motor-mouth tossed his cards on the table. "You want to know what I'm hiding? Nothing. My story is all over the TV." He strode to the door, opened it and knocked. "Oh, look. Nobody's there." His expression turned ugly. "Little girl who disappears. I'd take that any day over the bitch who shows up in my room and sets my bed on fire while I'm asleep. Yeah, it's just a nightmare, but when I wake up I smell like charcoal and there are burn holes in the sheet. Plus, my heart is racing so fast I swear I'm about to have a heart attack. Live with that and then complain to me about some mysterious little kid."

He slammed the door on his way out and the room shook.

"His story must be on True Crime," Preacher said. "It's five minutes to midnight. Where's your remote?"

I gave it to him and he turned on the television. He tuned to the news channel which I now knew broadcast more than just news and we caught the end of "True Crime." It wasn't Motor-mouth's story. It took me another month before I caught that. This program was over and was being summed up by its host, a young woman with long dark hair and sultry eyes.

She said: "His crime spree wouldn't have ended except for the stowaway witness. His life sentence without the possibility of parole has run out of appeals. The bodies of his last two victims were never found. For True Crime, this is Maheema Goruombi. Thanks for watching."

"Okay," Preacher said. "None of you are supposed to know about this, but . . ."

He pressed the menu button and up came a blue screen. Preacher punched in four digits and all of the sudden we had a connection to the universal web.

"How'd you learn about that?"

"Professional secrets," Preacher said as he found the "True Crime" website where any broadcast you wanted could be played. He searched the alphabetical listing of episodes until he came across one called, "Ladies on Fire."

It sounded promising and we watched.

It was about a sex slave enterprise and in the midst of it was our poker-playing pal, Motor-mouth. He'd been caught after a fire he'd accidentally set surfaced the operation. He'd managed to burn seven kidnapped women to death.

"I'm sorry I charred up some of the inventory. And I'm sorry I was caught." He displayed a sick, happy smile as he sat in a chair across from the reporter. He wore a hot magenta jumpsuit.

"What's he doing out?" Pipsqueak asked. "Did he escape? Or'd they release him?"

We had to watch to the end of the show to get our answer. He'd been sentenced before life expectancy had become what it was today and they'd had to release him while there was still a lot of breath in his body, so ruled the World Supreme Court. However, the epilogue said he was to be tried for other crimes.

Maybe that was my assignment. I was supposed to get close to him and get him to confess to other offenses so they could put him away. If that was the case, they should have said so because we all lost our taste for cards after that, and as far as I know, none of us ever saw Motor-mouth again. I don't know if he moved or what.

Time marched on. The housekeeper continued to try to talk to me and I did my best to avoid him. I started watching old movies. I preferred comedies, the stupider the better, but the stuff they broadcast was always scary and brooding. The little girl quit knocking at my door, which I was grateful for. But then this other thing started happening.

Every night around three a.m. I awoke to the sound of water running in the tub. I'd go check it out and the tub would be as dry as a bone. But then, this one night I went in and it's filled with water. I stood there staring until I heard that familiar knock at my door. After feeling like my feet were nailed to the floor, I moved to the peephole. What I saw chilled me to the core. She was looking up at me. Her nose a button. Her eyes round and wild. Her mouth open in a half moon grin, baby teeth confirming she was just a baby.

I think I stopped breathing for a minute. I certainly didn't open the door. I backed away and climbed into bed. She knocked all night and the water in the tub continued to spout. I stayed under the covers 'til morning. Didn't move a muscle 'til daylight. That's when the bathroom became quiet and she went away. I got up, went to the door and peeked out. She was gone. I went in the bathroom and looked at the tub. It was dry.

I didn't leave my room that day. I called room service feeling I needed food in my belly to settle my nerves.

When the delivery guy knocked, I knew it wasn't her, but naturally looked out the peephole anyway. I saw a close-up of someone's shirt so I opened the door.

Big Chum stood there with the same cat-swallowing-canary grin on his face the little girl'd had the night before. Water dripped from his hair. He extended a plate of food and said, "Would you like me to come in and explain about that pool now?"

I slammed the door in his face.

I was jelly-leg scared after that and I don't know how long I sat on the bed in a stupor. I was a body without a mind. I was a mass of neurons missing the correct receptors to allow me to move. I was a mess. It was night when I "woke up" and for all I knew, one day, two days, or even a month had passed.

I felt different than I had before. I was empty, listless, doped, exhausted—all those things. It was as if I'd been through something so terrifying I was too drained to even be afraid. And when the television came on of its own accord, I merely watched in a daze.

The narrator said, "True Crime. Two Deaths at Sea. The story of a daring con man who murdered people for their money. His last victims? A little girl with brown hair and her seven-foot-tall daddy."

Some cog in my brain began to turn.

Little girl. Big man. Little girl. Big man. Little girl. Big Chum . . .

That cog in my head turned more nimbly and got bigger cogs to move.

Was I being haunted because I'd let them drown? I'd failed to save them? That incident from ten years ago where the creep had slipped through my fingers. I hadn't given them justice so they were taking revenge?

Their pictures flickered on the screen. A loving father and his daughter. I stared, feeling more scared than sorry for them. I mean, they were haunting me and I was—

They showed my picture.

How could the show's producers know about me? Only my bosses knew I'd been trailing the con man.

That's when the fog began to lift. Something in my memory wasn't right. Irritation took hold. I rubbed my jaw. I rubbed so hard the skin on my hands felt raw from the stubble. I felt a headache coming on.

And then I had a realization that made it all clear.

My bad-guy-got-away story was a lie. He'd been caught. And now I knew. He was me.

Big Chum's real name was Roger Conroy and I'd chosen him to be my next mark. He had a boat for sale, a thirty-foot yacht called The Sainted Lady and I wanted it.

I posed as a buyer who wanted to be sure I was buying a well-maintained, top notch craft. Roger was pleased to show it off. We arranged a sailing date, just him and me. But then, surprise! He brought his little girl along.

I smiled at the child and mentioned something about how cute she was. What else could I say? She was there and I couldn't make an issue of it. I didn't want to delay the "transaction."

We took the boat out and when we were a good distance from shore, Roger cut the engine. It was a warm, sunny day. The sea was peaceful. Water lapped gently against the hull. I told him I wanted the boat. Relaxed and happy, he told me I was making a great deal.

"I couldn't agree with you more," I responded. The little girl giggled and smiled up at me.

He'd brought lunch for us and a six pack of beer. I waited until he was bent over, digging in the cooler, and then I made my move. I placed a stun gun to his shoulder and delivered two-hundred thousand volts. It dazed him enough for me to be able to cold-cock him.

The four-year-old screamed, "Don't hurt my daddy!"

I felt her tiny fists hitting my thigh as I handcuffed Roger. I grabbed her and slapped the two of them together. She was so squirmy I had to stun her with the gun before I could tie them up with nautical rope. Roger came to and she was fluttering her eyes just as I finished.

He started cussing at me, telling me what he was going to do when he got free. I ignored him and got busy bringing up the anchor. He kicked at me as I hooked it to the rope that had them tied. He knew what was coming and that was when his tune changed. He started begging for his life. "Don't do this. You don't have to do this. Please! She's just a little girl."

Never once did he make me want to change my mind because what could I do? The die had been cast. He shouldn't have sprung her on me. And I still wanted the boat. The most I can say is, I didn't smile as I watched them go over the side.

Now all I had to do was get back to shore and I could forge any documents I needed to sell The Sainted Lady. I would be a very rich man.

But I was in for a surprise. The four-year-old had a twelve-year-old stepbrother who was supposed to be home doing chores. Not wanting to miss out on the fun, he'd snuck on board and stowed away like a spy. If my timing had been different, if I'd just waited a smidge longer, I might have known he was there. But as it happened, I didn't, and he watched the whole thing. When I brought the boat back to shore, he wasted no time getting to his mother and told her what he'd witnessed.

The TV went off. Those cogs in my head slowed. I heard the water running in the tub and my heart went to pounding like a jackhammer. Something was up. Something was about to happen. The muscles in my face began to quiver as slowly, very slowly, I turned my head.

Big Chum and the little girl stood in the area outside the bathroom door.

I scrambled off the bed, lost my balance, and landed on all fours. I heard them coming toward me. There was no way I could get to my feet in time to get away. Besides, they were between me and the door and he was seven feet tall. I kept my head down. I couldn't look.

Something pressed against my shoulder and I heard a loud zapping sound as the electric current of a stun gun charged my nervous system. I lost control of my muscles. Nothing worked right.

Strong arms jerked me flat and rope was wrapped around my body. The next thing I knew, I was dragged into the bathroom where I lay on the cold tile floor. Water no longer flowed from the spigot of the tub and I knew it was full of water.

Petrified, unable to move my body, my mouth twitched and I found I could scream. Then: "Please. No. I'm sorry. I was wrong. Stop! Two wrongs don't make a right!" That last statement made Big Chum laugh as he lifted me up, dropped me in the tub, and these little-girl hands held me under.

So, here I am telling my story. You must be thinking that I didn't die. At first that's what I thought, too. I'd felt the pain of water entering my nose and filling my lungs before I blacked out. But here I was, alive and conscious, in the tub under the water.

I jerked up, gasping for breath, flopping like a fish until I was out of the tub, lying on my belly on the floor. I heard the sound one makes when gulping for air as my chest heaved. I was in a lot of pain. But after a while, the pain subsided and I just lay there, wondering what was going to happen next. In time I loosened the ropes and rolled onto my back.

It sounds dumb now, but after the ordeal I'd been through, I couldn't help but ask myself if I was dead. I had this idea that I was part of the hotel now. That I was a ghost destined to roam the halls of Skyglow for eternity.

I believed that outrageous thought for a few minutes before I realized I could feel my heartbeat. I stumbled out of the bathroom, stopping cold when I noticed an envelope had been slid under the door. I picked it up and read what was scribbled on the font: Read these and then come to the lobby.

I slipped pages of paper out of the envelope. They were stories. Four of them, all in my handwriting. I read. They were bizarre tales that all ended with my horrible death.

I went to the lobby and for the first time, the halls were filled with other guests of the Skyglow heading there as well. I didn't ask anyone what was going on. I just moved with the flow like an automaton.

I barely had time to take a seat when someone yelled, "Williams. In here." That was me, so I went through a door, into this office and there was my boss who'd given me the assignment in the first place.

"What's going on?" I asked.

"You don't know?"

I eyed him. I hadn't figured out a thing except maybe . . . I hesitated. "Does this place have ghosts?"

Now there was this other cop standing there and my boss looked at him and said, "Hasn't fully worn off."

The cop looked at his timepiece and answered, "Any time now."

"What?" I said. "What are you talking about?"

But they were silent and maybe a minute went by. I don't know because I was still kind of out of it. And then a thought hit me and I said the words, "Oh, God. Another year has passed."

"You know where you are now?" asked my boss.

I knew.

"You need me to fill you in on anything? Any holes in your memory?"

Lots of holes, but I wasn't sure I wanted them filled.

"You know what year it is?"

"Twenty-two-thirty-four," I answered.

"Five," he said.

Okay, five, I thought.

"You know how old you are?"

"One hundred ninety-four."

"You know how old they've calculated you will live?"

"I forget."

"Two hundred seventy-three. Genetics. You have a bad heart. The cigarettes can only do so much."

"Who wants to live that long in here anyway?"

"No one." He sort of smiled. "So what's your pleasure?"

"No!" I was irate. "Don't cut this short. This is one of the few times I get to spend with people in a lucid state. Explain it all to me again. That's the law. That's what you get paid the big bucks for."

My boss, or rather the warden I knew now, looked at the other cop and then he said, "This is Skyglow Prison. It used to be a hotel. Most of the big centuries-old hotels are used as prisons nowadays. There's not a lot of room to build new modern facilities. And no money."

"And the law says you can't kill me," I added.

"No. We can't kill you. Capital punishment was outlawed a century ago, but of course, society still breeds killers. Got to put you somewhere."

"And . . ." I was going to make him say it.

"And what?"

"The law was changed . . ."

"The law was changed so that there are no more recreation yards or weight rooms. Not for people like you who really do deserve death."

"But you get to do cruel and unusual."

"Not at all. It's been argued all the way to the Supreme World Court, appealed twenty different ways. Any cruelty you experience is of your mind's own making. And the punishment may be unusual, but it has been ruled humane. That unusual provision written way back when was meant to thwart bizarre, painful stuff."

"I experienced bizarre, painful stuff."

"That your mind created."

"So, I killed these people once. Why should I have to die over and over again?"

"You don't have to. It's your own mind punishing you. We just give you the shot that scrambles your brain for one year. You live the life your brain creates, within the confines of this prison, of course. And if you don't like the scenario your brain comes up with, you have a choice."

"I don't have to take the shot. I can vegetate in my room for a year."

"That's right."

"And I can't change my mind once the year has begun."

"Right again."

"Even though I may go stark raving mad."

"I think that's an exaggeration."

"You've never experienced it."

He shrugged.

"You've tried it both ways. Every year it's back and forth. Can't take the solitary, you opt for the dream. Can't take your own mind's punishment, you opt for solitary. It's not our fault if you don't go for the third option. Of course, only one in forty thousand do."

"What third option? What are you talking about?"

"You have to figure that out for yourself."

I searched my brain for what he could possibly mean.

"What are you going to do this year?"

I stared at him. Both options were hell. What was this third choice he'd mentioned? I reviewed everything that had happened over the past year. I even thought about the stories I'd written covering those other years. The people I met were always different. Preacher, Pipsqueak, and Motor-mouth weren't in any of those other nightmares.

And then I realized. The housekeeper was. What about him? I pictured his face. Friendly. Chatty. He always wanted to talk about me. And his energy always felt like it was encroaching. Like it was trying to change me. *Transform* me! That was it. What was it he'd said? *You're the master of your own destiny.*

I got it now. He was my conscience. And if I could really change, really understand, really repent . . . What then? Would I stop drowning myself or shooting myself or burying myself alive?

I smiled and the warden seemed to know what I was thinking.

"I should tell you there has been a new development. The legislature passed a law. Starting now, you are only allowed to repent five years before you die. So the formula in the elixir we give has been changed."

"That's not right."

"Do-gooders keep you alive. Not-so-do-gooders make sure you're punished."

"But I have seventy-nine years to go. I only killed six people."

"That we were able to prove."

Okay, eleven, I thought without going into particulars of how I'd snuffed out each one.

"And you would have killed more. For money. Their yachts. Their property. Their bank accounts."

"I didn't make enough as a cop."

"You were never a cop, you sniveling piece of crap."

He looked like he wanted to come at me from across the desk. "But you killed one," he snarled. "And left a gun by his side trying to make him look like the bad guy."

Oh, yeah. That shot they gave me had really scrambled my brain.

"You're a sick-o scumbag and I'm tired of talking to you. Living in this rat hole is better than you deserve. Now you get to choose. So choose."

"What about—"

"Shot? Or no shot?"

"Give me a minute," I said, thinking, *One minute. One glorious, real minute where what I see is real and I know I'm truly alive.*

"Choose. Then you sit over there and write about the past year before you go back to your cell."

I felt my eyes grow hot with tears and snot welled inside my nose.

"Sniveler," the cop said.

Sniveler? He was right. I was the sniveler. I did this every year when it came time to make my decision because I was never ready and I had to make it quick. If I didn't, they would make it for me.

"This time," I said and I paused as I saw a tear splash onto my hand. I wiped it away. "This time I guess I choose . . ."

Made in the USA
Middletown, DE
09 May 2022

65417196R00050